Find Me In Paradise

an adventure with romance

Deb Gardner Allard

Deb Allard Books

Ferrysburg, MI

Deb Allard Books
debgardnerallard@everydayromancewithdeb.com

Book Layout © 2023 BookDesignTemplates.com
Book cover designer: Marianne Nowicki

Songs mentioned in the novel:
"At Last," sung by Etta James, written by Mack Gordon and Harry Warren. RCA, 1941.
"Come Away with Me," written and sung by Nora Jones. Blue Note Records, 2002.
"Can't Help Falling in Love," sung by Elvis Presley, written by Hugh Peretti, Luigi Creatore, and George David Weiss, publisher, Gladys Music, Inc., producer, Elvis Presley. RCA Victor 1961.
"Perfect," written and sung by Ed Sheeran, 2017. Producer, Ed Sheeran. Asylum Atlantic.
"Just the Way You Are," written and sung by Billy Joel, 1977, Columbia label.

Find Me In Paradise/ Deb Gardner Allard--1st ed.
Paperback ISBN: 979-8-218-34389-7

Dedication

To Him who watches over my coming and going. May I never spend a day without your guidance.

"Because you are my help, I sing in the shadow of your wings."

—PSALM 63:7 NIV

And to Brian, Rachel, Allison, Aaron, Pat, and Martha Jr. for your support and encouragement. Lindsay, your brilliant suggestions wow'd me. I'll keep you all supplied with toffee butterscotch cookies whenever you're ready!

About the Book

Adventure meets romance and suspense in *Find Me In Paradise*—about a disastrous colleague vacation in the Caribbean.

After landing safely in Scarlett Bay for a colleague vacation, a twist of fate separates Sloan from her resort. When she awakens in an unfamiliar room with a deep voice speaking behind a screen, her heart nearly pounds from her chest. *Who is the man and why won't he show himself?* Before long, she senses he's hiding something more chilling than she can imagine. Can she escape before it's too late?

Back in St. Anne's Landing, the surgeon she secretly loves learns of her failure to check into the Las Palmeras resort and quickly charters a private jet to Scarlett Bay. On reaching the resort, Rob receives a staff member's recommendation to hire the crusty, larger-than-life Detective Delroy, an ex-body builder and ex-police officer to help him locate Sloan. But Delroy doesn't appear capable of surviving lunch, let alone conducting a search.

As the seconds tick by for finding Sloan alive, Rob hires Delroy, but soon discovers the detective's shoddy transportation and habit of sleeping until noon seriously hinder their efforts. Despite the ever-increasing obstacles, will Rob find the woman he loves in the raging Caribbean Sea, which harbors over seven-thousand islands, sharks, and a slew of shady characters?

It won't matter if the mysterious recluse of Paradise Island has his way. If Jameson can suppress Sloan's memories long enough, he might accomplish his plans, but only if she doesn't flee after uncovering his worst, most terrifying secrets—secrets

that will shatter her world and leave her reeling from the truth about Paradise Island.

Author's Note

Dear Reader, I hope this tropical adventure grips your heart in ways you might not expect. Maybe you'll fret over the savvy doctor or the mysterious recluse while fearing for Sloan. It's justified, but swallow your donut and grip your pillow before the climax because it's gonna be good—and don't say I didn't warn you.

Chapter One

December 26, 2016

Sloan had a question for Dr. Rob Ambrose, the most sought-after bachelor in Marysville, but asking it required perfect timing. Her breath misted the frigid air as she stood on her apartment's sidewalk and watched him emerge from his Bronco. "You're on time!" she shouted.

"Yep, the life of a surgeon, right?" Dr. Rob Ambrose slid across the street's black ice on his trek to the curb.

He unbuttoned his trendy suit jacket and adjusted the skinny silver tie around his neck when he neared her. She couldn't believe she was about to travel with her boss to the Caribbean. Their unmarried cardiac patients would have meltdowns if they knew. They gossiped like busybodies over his every move, each one longing for a date. Sloan smiled imagining them begging for details on her return.

She glanced at her clothing, a casual spandex top and flouncy Boho skirt under her unbuttoned coat. They were stark contrasts to his sharp attire. But she loved his polished look, even if it was a bit excessive for plane travel. Heck, she'd sacrifice a week of creamy caramel lattes to leap into his arms and smother him in kisses, but unfortunately, theirs was more of a doctor/nurse, pass the chart please relationship where they chatted during lunch hours with their clinic coworkers. She sighed just thinking about it.

Rob swept the dark locks from his eyes as he stepped to the curb. "You look beautiful, Sloan."

Really? She bit her tongue to keep from shouting, *You look drop dead gorgeous, doctor.* Instead, she settled for a less exuberant, "You don't look bad either," but heat spread over her cheeks, betraying her true feelings.

"Here, let me take your luggage." He hoisted her suitcase and travel bag into the Bronco's trunk, then shivered while rubbing his arms. "Ready to get this trip on the road?"

"Sure am."

He offered her his hand to the Bronco's passenger door before weaving around to the driver's side. Sloan reflected on the times she'd flirted with him between patients at the clinic. He hadn't seemed to notice until out of nowhere, he began inviting her for an occasional coffee at the Royal Brew or a maple donut at Adele's Corner Bakery after work. Nothing fancy and not technically dates either. She'd had the impression they were merely friends sharing rides until he asked her to call him *Rob* instead of doctor. But...did it mean she was more than his coffee and donut pal? She'd spent half the night pondering that dilemma.

Before she realized it, the Bronco entered the airport's dusky parking lot and braked under a light post. When Rob opened the passenger door, she extended her legs from the vehicle.

"You seem more mature, more savvy with your hair down," he said. His Ambrose dimple deepened as he offered her his hand.

Every thought in her head turned to mush. With their clinic closed for the Christmas holidays, he'd surprised her and their coworkers with a seven-day, all-expenses-paid vacation to the Caribbean...and now, he'd complimented her twice.

"Are you okay?" he added when she didn't respond. "You're rarely this quiet or...tight-lipped."

Did he think she had tight lips? It wasn't the relaxed look she was going for. She accepted his hand and stepped to the pavement. "I'm fine." But her strained voice suggested otherwise.

In his compassionate way, Rob placed his hands on her shoulders. "What's going on?"

"I, uh..." Another whiff of his sweet cologne, and she'd melt into a pool of distractions centered on his mesmerizing blue eyes. But there wasn't time for more daydreaming.

"You're not having second thoughts about Scarlett Bay, are you?" Rob's voice, barely above a whisper, carried a slight tremor.

"N–no. It's not that." It was anything but that.

He peered at her through what she imagined were the dreamy portals of his soul. "I was saving this for a special occasion, but I can't wait. There's something I've wanted to ask you for weeks, but my past is rather complicated. I've had to put...certain things to rest.

The wheels spun in Sloan's mind, releasing a million thoughts. "What is it, Rob?" Every second he lingered for words seemed like hours.

He backed against the Bronco and drew her close. "Would you...mind if I..." He lowered his head, his wintergreen breath warming her lips, feathery light, followed by—

Three teenage boys stopped at the SUV's bumper and gawked at them. The skyscraper with enormous sneakers and wild blond hair planted his hands on his hips. "Don't be lame, dude. Kiss her."

"Oh, yeah?" With a twinkle in his eyes, Rob gathered snow from the car beside him and hurled a snowball at the teen.

The boy brushed the slush from his parka and turned back. "Is that all you've got, bro?" He and the other two boys scooped snow from a nearby car and began pelting Rob.

"Oh, I see. Snow wars." Using the car as a shield, Rob returned the barrage. After a few rounds, he chuckled and planted his palms in the air. "Okay. Okay. Truce. I have a plane to catch."

"Yeah, we have to pick up our parents." The skyscraper wiped his hands on his parka again. "Oh, and you might wanna learn some better moves, dude." He sprinted toward the terminal with the other teens.

Rob glanced sheepishly at Sloan. "We'd better head inside." He removed their suitcases from the trunk and extended the handles.

Stalling, she dusted his coat. "I was wondering what you wanted to ask me?" *Was it to marry him?* She chuckled under her breath at how she'd moved him from dating material to marriage license in less than an hour.

"Never mind." An impish grin parted his lips. "My timing was off."

Sloan's imagination ran wild as she gripped their luggage handles. Had she been imagining things, or had he almost kissed her? A surge of courage suddenly replaced her doubts. "Wait, Rob, I need to ask you something too."

He closed the trunk and shouldered their travel bags. "Would you mind saving it for the plane? We need to hurry." He power-walked through the parking lot, Sloan at his side, trying to keep up with his long strides.

The St. Anne's City Airport was free of hustle and bustle in the Monday predawn hours. Apart from Sloan and Rob, only a few people stood in the check-in line. After confirming their tickets, handing over luggage, and going through security, they headed to the gate. Sloan's sister Vivi, their cardiology clinic receptionist, rose from her seat near the boarding tunnel when they rounded the corner.

"Hi, Viv." Sloan glanced around the waiting area. Several of their coworkers had delayed their trip, but the gated area was empty save for Viv.

A uniformed gate attendant raised a handheld device to her lips. "Last call for passengers boarding Flight 229 to Atlanta. I repeat, last call for passengers boarding Flight 229 to Atlanta."

The plane had boarded?

Rob's cell phone rang. "Wait a minute, Sloan." He removed the device from his suit pocket.

"Please don't answer it." She slipped her travel bag from his arm and swung it over her shoulder.

He checked the caller ID. "I wish I didn't have to."

Sloan understood, but the timing couldn't be worse. Two rings later, Rob accepted the call.

"Hello?" A few seconds passed before he covered the phone. "Go ahead, ladies. I'll be there soon."

Vivi hustled through the boarding tunnel, but Sloan turned back for one more glance at the man she adored. *What had he wanted to ask her?*

Chapter Two

Rob paced the empty gate area with his cell phone. He'd waited for his home to sell for months, and now, an over-eager buyer wanted the transaction to occur immediately. Why couldn't he wait for another seven days or handle everything online? Reasoning with the realtor on the phone was like trying to convince a sixty-year-old to stop eating French fries for the sake of her arteries.

"I'm sorry, ma'am, but it's impossible." How could he make her understand he didn't have time to argue? "I'm about to board a plane for an important vacation."

"The home buyer is old-fashioned." Mrs. Bekker raised her usually calm voice. "He insists on the paperwork taking place at the bank. In person. And he's offering an extra million to seal the deal quickly. Something about a business trip to Europe."

The weighty offer tempted Rob. He could use the funds to pay off debts and his new home. But was the extra money worth delaying his trip to Scarlett Bay? No. He had something special planned for the irresistible, long-legged Sloan. Given the horrible event defining his past, he hoped he might have a second chance at love. "I'm sorry, Mrs. Bekker, but I have to catch my flight."

He glanced at the broad-shouldered gate attendant who paid him no mind. She gripped the jet bridge door and pulled it closed.

"Stop!" he shouted. *Was the attendant blind?* How could she not notice he was on an important phone call? "I have to go," he told Mrs. Bekker.

He pocketed the phone and dashed to the tunnel door. "Please let me through, ma'am. There's someone waiting for me on the plane."

The attendant barred the door and stood firm. "Sorry, sir. I gave the last calls for boarding."

"But I have to get on that plane."

"Unfortunately, you can't. The pilot is preparing for takeoff."

"But I rented an expensive celebration room. Our friends will be there." He fished in his suit coat for his cell phone and called Sloan.

Her "Be Happy" tune rang nearby, and a sick feeling swept over him. "That's my friend's phone."

The gate attendant retrieved the boisterous device from the floor and flipped it over in her hand. "Hmm. She must have dropped it before boarding."

Rob ran to the adjacent floor-to-ceiling windows. "Come on, Sloan, look out a window." He waved his arms overhead and searched the glass portals on the plane's midsection. But the dim morning light veiled his ability to see her.

The gate attendant tilted her head to her shoulder without blinking. "Sir, she can't hear you."

Obviously, but somehow shouting his thoughts eased the thumping tachycardia threatening to rip open his chest. "You don't understand, ma'am. I hurried to the gate so we'd be early. I'm never late for—for anything. Please, can't you make an exception?" He thumped the glass with his palm. "Please, Sloan, look out the window."

The no-nonsense attendant lifted a rectangular device to her lips, her eyes fixed on him. "Code Bravo, Gate 15. I repeat. Code Bravo, Gate 15." She glared at Rob as if he were the knife-wielding lunatic in Psycho. "Step away from the glass, sir."

Rob couldn't believe what was happening. He was a surgeon, a pillar in the community, not a social deviant.

Two lofty airport policemen rounded the corner and charged the gate. Decked in uniforms with badges, they raced around the roped barrier and past the seating area.

"Is he the trouble?" The taller policeman directed his chin at Rob.

Rob glanced both ways before thumbing his chest. "Surely you're not referring to me?"

The policeman nodded.

Rob twisted for a glance over his shoulder. The gate remained empty except for the four of them.

The attendant, who had her arm propped at her waist, screwed her lips into a tiny o, as she raised one eye at the officers and moved her finger in and out at Rob.

She obviously hadn't understood his plight! At least there weren't reporters nearby. Because of his Ambrose family's prestige in the community, anything involving them often made the news in St. Anne's Landing. Rob imagined the headlines: "Cardiothoracic Surgeon, Dr. Robert Harrington Ambrose of St. Anne's Landing, Ousted from City Airport."

The policemen, now hugging his sides, slipped their arms under his and dragged him, bucking and shouting, "Let me go!" past the gate area and through the security checkpoint. But even worse, several travelers snapped pictures and videotaped the event with their cell phones. He'd make the evening news for sure.

Sloan's heart-shaped face flashed through his mind. What had she wanted to ask him?

Chapter Three

The connecting flight from Atlanta to Scarlett Bay landed, and after waiting in line, Sloan descended the outside steps attached to the plane's cabin. Her sister, Vivi, stood below her on the tarmac gazing at the tropical scenery along the runway. The plush greenery accented a cerulean sky more beautiful than any Sloan had ever seen. She only wished Rob was here to see it.

Rampant thoughts of what kept him from boarding the plane prompted a one-track mind—finding her cell phone. *Had she lost it?* It wasn't in her travel bag. She steered Vivi to the air terminal after they collected their luggage. A young blonde with dreadlocks intercepted them on the way. "Hello, ladies! You need ride?" She waved a cardboard taxi sign.

Sloan contemplated her need to call Rob before responding, "Thank you, maybe later." She bypassed the cabbie and headed into the terminal with her sister.

"Whoa." Viv spun around. "What happened to the walls?"

A cement floor covered in dirt and an accordion-fold metal ceiling accounted for what the travel brochure called "the Scarlett Bay Air Terminal." Over their heads, large fan blades wobbled, creating a clatter as they struggled to produce a breeze. Despite the primitive surroundings, people from many nationalities milled about the place adorned in vivid lime, orange, and fuchsia-pink garb. They carried items for sale, including long-stemmed white roses and shirts printed with exotic birds, leafy fronds, and tropical flowers. Coconut and pineapple scents infused the air, tempting perspiring tourists to hand over money before sipping drinks trimmed with paper umbrellas.

Sloan spotted a young man selling pink orchids. "Excuse me, sir. Can you direct us to a tourist information booth?"

"Si, señorita. Through there." He nodded at a dense crowd of boisterous travelers.

Sloan and Vivi sidled through the mob until they spotted a brightly lit booth beneath a canvas information banner. A sunbaked woman sporting a pink rose behind her ear drummed the wooden countertop with her painted fingertips. She popped a peppermint into her mouth as Sloan approached her with questions.

"Time to resort?" the lady responded. "Depends on how you travel. And phone call?" She waved to what some might have considered a stairway. "Follow those steps to taxis. Phone booth down there too."

"Thank you." Sloan wheeled her luggage to the cracked cement steps littered with upended concrete chunks. She and Vivi navigated the obstacle course to the lower level, where more islanders wagged *taxi* signs.

"Hey, remember me?" The same cabbie with blonde dreadlocks and neon yellow shirt wagged her sign. "I give you ride. Come. Go with me."

Sloan appreciated the blonde's determination since this floor delivered scruffier drivers, but the gal's rusty, paint-chipped taxi, a jumble of colors, caused Sloan to hesitate. "Our travel agent mentioned a van or plane. Can you tell us where those are?"

"Sure. Sure. I drive you wherever you want. You going to resort?" The cabbie's relaxed smile appeared friendly enough.

"Uh, wait a minute," Sloan said. She reached into her travel bag and produced a brochure. "Here it is. The Las Palmeras."

"I see. Van ride take four hours. Plane ride shorter."

"Four hours?" Sloan huddled with her sister. "Should we take the plane?"

"Let's fly," Viv said with certainty.

"Great. Now, where's a phone?" Sloan eagle-eyed the busy terminal, but had no idea what to look for.

The blonde led them to an unoccupied glass-enclosure on a wall. Wasting no time, Sloan called Rob. His cellular rang, but a recording announced the message box was full. *Great. What were the odds?*

"No luck," she told Viv. Her knees nearly buckled as she walked to the taxi.

"You look pale, Sloan. Let me help you." Vivi opened the sedan's back door and assisted her inside before heading to the opposite side.

Humming an unrecognizable tune, the cabbie placed their suitcases in the trunk and slid into the driver's seat. "You two ready?" she asked.

Sloan nodded, but seconds later, she let out a screech. "What in the...my foot fell through the floor!"

The cabbie didn't act the least bit surprised. "It was bound to happen soon." She returned to starting the car.

Biting her tongue, Sloan straddled the gaping hole and scanned the jagged rips in the seats and the faded lemon air freshener dangling from the rearview mirror. The vehicle seemed a bit shoddy for a tourist ride.

As the cabbie adjusted her rearview mirror, baby powder and canned ravioli scents wafted through the cab. She glanced in the mirror at Sloan before stepping on the gas. "I'm Makenna, but call me Mac."

Sloan had no other choice but to suck up her fears over their safety. "I was wondering where you got this car, Mac?" It was a valid question, considering...

The cabbie eyed her in the rearview mirror again before expanding her chest as though filled with pride. "From the best junkyard in Scarlett Bay."

The island's junkyard served as a used car dealership? The taxi's tires hit a deep pothole, and Sloan's head banged the window. "Ow!"

"Sorry, lady." Genuine empathy softened Mac's tone.

Sloan rubbed her aching temple but clamped her mouth to keep from groaning. A distinct possibility existed that Rob had selected the wrong tropical island for their vacation. Someone should have verified the amenities.

"Taxi ain't pretty, but it gives me work." Mac cleared her throat. "You two sure about going to small airport?"

"Is there a problem?" Sloan met the cabbie's eyes in the mirror.

The blonde made a sour face. "It's just..." she began. "There's something creepy about the place. Gives me the chills."

"What do you mean?" Sloan leaned closer to the front.

Mac's voice lowered. "People fly outta there and don't come back. But I'll drive you to Las Palmeras for a small fee—only two thousand dollars."

What? Was she delirious? Sloan would've liked to help the poverty-stricken lady, but her price was tourist robbery. "Thanks for the offer, but we'll stick with the plane."

Mac slammed her foot on the gas, and the car clattered past palm trees, white, purple, and pink flowers, rusted cars, and run-down wooden houses resembling sheds until Mac lifted a finger from the steering wheel. "Small airport over there."

Sloan craned her neck out the window. *Did she mean the rundown building big enough for two small planes?*

"That's it?" Vivi asked.

"What you expect?" Mac swerved the taxi into a parking space by the building.

Sloan shook her head. She'd given up on expectations after her foot fell through the floor. She climbed from the cab with Vivi while Mac removed their wheeled luggage from the trunk.

Up ahead, a small plane rested on a lifeless tarmac. A lanky young fellow wearing a striped Rastafarian hat over ginger hair strolled toward them. As he approached, his flowery shirt emitted an overwhelming sweat cologne. Mac shot him what appeared to be a knowing grin about something, but it didn't faze Sloan, given Scarlett Bay's size. They were probably related.

The flashy man bowed to Sloan and Vivi with his hand covering his heart. "How dee do. Trinidad, pilot, at your service. Wherever you need fly, Trinidad your guy, for five hundred bucks, that is." He directed his gaze at the plane parked on the runway.

The aircraft possessed more rust than the taxi cab. Sloan set her travel bag on the tarmac. "We're going to the Las Palmeras."

"Ah. Short ride up, short ride down, twenty minutes tops." Trinidad used hand motions as he spoke. "We be there quick. Besides, I fly low."

His little puddle jumper resembled a vintage WWII plane Sloan had seen in a movie. She was brilliant at creating scenarios from horror films, but this wasn't the moment to put nightmarish thoughts into Vivi's head.

"Should we fly?" She hoped her sister wouldn't mind. Reaching the resort and calling Rob was all she could think about.

"I'm not sure." Viv gathered her hair into a ponytail and secured it with the decorative lavender band Sloan had gifted her before the trip. "Going by van might be safer," Viv said.

"No, no, no. Van ride take four hours. You be sorry. Scary ride around mountain cliffs." In a cocky manner, Trinidad removed the sunglasses tucked in his tropical shirt and flipped them over his bloodshot eyes, but Sloan noted the redness. Was the man lacking sleep or, heaven forbid, strung out on drugs? As a nurse, she had concerns.

The pilot seemed to notice her staring at him. He glanced at the ground and placed his hands in his pockets. "Not to worry. Trinidad under the weather but can fly anywhere, any day, any time."

Could he be trusted? Sloan had doubts, but where would she find another pilot? She ascended the plane's steps and peeked inside the cabin, where perspiration and pepperoni pizza fumes swam up her nose as she inspected the duct-taped seats and the missing pilot and front passenger doors.

Hmm, maybe flying wasn't such a great idea. On the positive side, Trinidad stated he'd fly low, and she and Vivi were skilled swimmers if they had to dive. He also insisted the flight would be short, which was Sloan's number one reason for taking the plane. But on the negative side…she bit her lip and shivered.

Behind her on the steps, Vivi stretched her neck to see into the cabin. "This thing looks like it's ready for the La Brea Tar Pits."

Sloan elbowed her sister. "In case you didn't know, the tar pits aren't for dumping."

"That's not the point," Vivi said. "This contraption could have flown Amelia Earhart."

Trinidad walked to the steps and leaned on the handrail. "Plane not *that* old. Thieves stole doors. But it make same flight earlier today. No problem. I fly so low, you can jump in water. We go now."

Second thoughts pestered Sloan, but she removed money from a pouch in her travel bag and clutched it while watching Mac's cab and its noisy muffler sputter away.

After it disappeared, Sloan turned to Trinidad. "Are you sure this thing is safe?"

Chapter Four

Rob collapsed in the Bronco, his head planted on the steering wheel. How had things gone so wrong? He should have handed the gate attendant his ticket while talking on the phone, and he should have listened when Sloan tried to tell him whatever she had to share in the parking lot. Had she been trying to back out of the vacation? His temples throbbed from rehashing every detail.

He had to stop berating himself.

Speaking into his car phone, he called his housekeeper. "Paley, could you please book a ticket for the next flight to Scarlett Bay?"

"Of course, Rob, but weren't you supposed to leave this morning?"

"Long story. I'll fill you in when I'm not on the road."

He ended the call as the highway ramp to Marysville came into view. Eager to find joy in his joyless day, he drove to the builder's office for his soon-to-be new home and obtained a key.

He'd been grieving his wife's death for three long years before Sloan joined the Addington group at the Marysville Cardiology Clinic. Eating with his coworkers in the clinic lunchroom had helped him get to know them. He'd felt drawn to Sloan's kind heart, but he lacked the nerve to ask her on a date despite encouragement from family and friends. A few months ago, he began inviting her to "tag along" on his usual after-work stops. He made the outings sound like no big deal, as though sparing her from driving herself for coffee and donuts.

If only he knew how the glossy-haired beauty felt about him. With Vivi's help, he had arranged and paid for the coworkers' vacations to Scarlett Bay with a plan to date Sloan. But he hadn't told Vivi his intent.

As he rounded the corner, he spotted the two-story home that was almost his. It couldn't be more perfect for his needs. He parked in the paved driveway, unlocked the thick oak door, and walked through the foyer to the living room. Fresh paint and new carpet scents laced the air. From the living room, he strolled to the open kitchen and imagined conversing with Sloan in the adjoining family room while he made a snack on the kitchen island.

The cozy house was far different from his parents' mansion. He expected a new life with a difficult adjustment period. For starters, who ever heard of a Marysville country doctor rocking on the front porch in Ralph Lauren? He'd have to ditch his designer clothing and alter his lifestyle. He was ready for it if Sloan agreed to marry him. But how would he pay for the home if his mansion didn't sell?

An idea came to mind, and he called Mrs. Bekker. "I missed the flight today, so I can sign the paperwork—if you make it happen."

"I'm on it," she said and ended the call.

After the closing, Rob planned to call an interior designer to transform the new place into a cozy country home for Sloan, born and raised in rural Marysville.

Peering out the kitchen window, he imagined coming home to a golden retriever named J.R.R. after Tolkien.

Of course, he'd call him J.R. He'd sit by the hearth and stroke the pup's fur. They'd play fetch, walk through the woods, and play rough and tumble on the living room carpet. As an only child, Rob had dreamed of owning a dog and having a house filled with little ones.

Little ones. He was already in his mid-thirties and couldn't afford to waste time before starting a family. Setting his dreams aside, he left his soon-to-be home, returned the key, and drove the route to his apartment in St. Anne's Landing for some downtime.

His pager buzzed as his thoughts veered to which medical journal might arrive in the mail today. He asked Siri to call the number. "This is Dr. Ambrose," he announced to the caller.

"Dr. Amey Jhara, here. We have an emergency. Chest pain unrelieved by medication. Imaging shows a blockage. Dr. Addington is in surgery on another case. Can you get here ASAP?"

"I'll be there in less than ten." Rob swerved to the off-ramp and listened as Dr. Jhara shared more details.

True to his vow, Rob parked in the physician's lot and dashed to the Cath lab in under ten minutes. Pushing worries aside, he dashed to the nurse's station and checked the vital signs, lab work, and imaging reports before examining the patient. The man needed an immediate angioplasty.

Rob changed into surgical gear, scrubbed, and entered the procedure room. Blocking all worries from his mind, he focused on the patient.

The procedure was a success. The patient might survive for many years, barring unforeseeable events.

He wrote post-procedure orders in the recovery room, then called Dr. Addington, who agreed to assume the patient's care.

Worried about Sloan and Vivi, Rob walked to the locker room, changed into his suit, and searched for his phone. His coworkers should have landed by now.

He found the phone where he'd left it in his inner suit pocket. No messages. But a long-distance number appeared under recent calls. A scammer? He received more than his fair share every day. Why hadn't Sloan called him on Vivi's phone? Perhaps he was right; she didn't want a relationship. It would hurt deeply, but maybe he could convince her in Scarlett Bay to give him another chance.

He exhaled long and hard then called Paley. "I'm sorry, Rob," she said. "There aren't any flights available to Scarlett Bay for the next two days."

The beep of an incoming call interrupted them. "I'll have to get back to you, Paley." He ended the call and accepted the new one.

"Rob, I've done all sorts of figure eights to make the home closings happen today so you can fly to the Caribbean, and the buyer can leave for Italy, but you'll need to arrive at the bank by 4 p.m." Mrs. Bekker's harried tone encouraged him to get moving.

He dashed out of the locker room with the phone to his ear. "Thank you, ma'am." His watch showed 3:20. There wasn't enough time, but he'd defy the odds and make it anyway.

Chapter Five

S loan inspected the plane again. Flying in the old contraption might be a reckless decision. Knowing sensible Dr. Rob, he'd steer them to the taxi if he were present. Still, she supposed it wasn't much scarier than hang gliding, which she'd only watched from shore.

"Puddle jumper flew to resort early today. No problem. Besides, I fly low." Trinidad's insistent, cheery tone eased Sloan's worries the teensiest bit.

She and Vivi had worked as lifeguards at their community pool during high school summers, so if the plane developed a problem, diving into the sea and swimming to shore was an option.

She handed Trinidad the money, which he tucked in his shirt pocket. Yanking his red and yellow striped hat over his ginger hair, he edged past them into the cockpit, hopped into the pilot seat, and studied the switches. Vivi climbed into the back, and Sloan opted for the doorless front passenger seat to keep Viv safe from the opening. "Hey, Trinidad, where's the seatbelt?"

"Over there." He gestured behind Sloan's head.

"You mean this old duffle strap?"

"That's it."

"When was this thing built?"

"Uh, ten, twenty..." He turned his head in the opposite direction and coughed. "Sixty years ago."

Was the broken-down plane older than her adoptive father?

"Seatbacks double as flotation pads. See? Push here." Trinidad glanced at Sloan, then behind her at Vivi.

Flotation pads? Fear, panic, reality. Sloan's hands shook like an unbalanced car wheel as the plane's engine rattled alive. Would Rob call this playing Russian Roulette with her life? She and Vivi needed to abort their decision. The four-hour van ride around cliffs couldn't be worse than the fear clawing at her gut to exit while there was still time.

She leaned back for Vivi to hear. "We need to get off the plane."

But the puddle jumper sputtered, drowning her words. It headed down the runway, wobbling over the tarmac, picking up speed. Sloan shouted at the top of her lungs, "I changed my mind. Stop the plane. We have to get off." But the rickety craft rose into the air.

"See. Plane safe." Trinidad glanced at her, his smile revealing a gold-capped tooth.

"How long is this trip?" she shouted over the clanging noise.

"Like I say earlier, twenty minutes tops. Settle back. Enjoy ride."

Enjoy? ENJOY? While hanging on for her ever-loving life to avoid being hurled through the doorless portal into the sea? She glanced at the waves. The deep blue curls complemented the sky. Enormous sea turtles swam beneath the frothy surface away from the shore.

"Sloan, look! It's beautiful down there." Vivi's excitement distracted Sloan from her fears.

Trinidad glanced in the back. "You keep watching. See Las Palmeras soon."

Seagulls dotted the sky, and a massive fish with a dorsal fin sprang from the water and disappeared into the deep. "Did you see the shark?" Vivi's squeal electrified the cabin.

Sloan had seen the fin, too, before it dove beneath the sea.

Trinidad stretched over her lap and peered through her door frame. "Could be shark. Or dolphin."

"It was a shark. Definitely a shark. I've seen them in aquariums." Vivi returned to her window view as Trinidad studied his control panel.

Without warning, smoke spewed from the wings and dissipated before Sloan's eyes. Was something wrong? Her overactive imagination aroused thoughts of the Devil's Triangle. Were they near it? Could they be sucked into a massive whirlpool and meet their dooms? "Please tell me we're not in the Bermuda Triangle."

"No way." As the pilot spoke, his fingers scrambled over the control panel.

More smoke billowed into the sky and clouded the plane's windshield. A melted metal odor and a nasty oil stench saturated the cockpit. "What's going on?" Vivi yelled from the back.

"Not to worry. Just an oil leak. Stay calm." Shaking like a first-time flyer, Trinidad appeared anything but calm.

"Just an oil leak? How do you fix an oil leak in the air?" Sloan glanced over her shoulder and spotted smoke rolling like a giant beach ball behind the plane.

"Everything okay. No need to worry. Dang engine." Trinidad studied the control panel as if the blaring red alarm would tell him what to do.

"Engine? Did you say engine? The motor for the plane?" Sloan eyed the water before scooting to the inner edge of her seat. She clawed at the leather cording and stretched her seatbelt to the max. Should she and Vivi dive from the craft into the sea and save themselves? They were still too high in the air. Wait—they'd spotted a shark, too. But on the other hand—the engine might die. "Hey, what happened to your accent, Trinidad?"

"Harvard grad. Can't talk now." Sweat poured from his forehead like rain as he glanced at the controls.

Harvard? Was he a tropical imposter? "I don't care what you are. Fly the plane." Using every ounce of strength she could muster, Sloan clenched her teeth to stop them from chattering as Trinidad frantically fingered every lever on the control panel. "Wait, you're not a pilot either, are you?"

"Aced my online class."

"What?" Sloan released the edge of her seat and braced the ceiling, her body tremors topping the Richter scale. "Grab your floatation pad, Viv!"

"Got it," she shouted, her voice bursting with panic.

Sloan tore at hers. Her knuckles scraped the patched leather as she ripped it loose, hitting herself in the nose and smearing blood on the cushion.

Trinidad struggled to keep the plane in a steady glide, but within seconds, he lost control. More shrieks filled the cabin, the loudest one from Trinidad.

"Hold on, Viv!" Sloan shouted.

Dark smoke blanketed the windshield, and the water below came closer and closer...

Chapter Six

The trip to the bank would take forty minutes. Rob checked his watch. 3:30. The meeting was at 4 p.m. Would ten minutes kill the deal? He'd drive the quick route and hope the bridge wasn't icy. He entered his vehicle and headed from the hospital parking lot to I-95.

The speedometer flickered past the speed limit. He eased off the gas pedal. The gargantuan Bridge Conditions sign, a mile from the Grand River Bridge, illuminated an electronic message: Prepare for backups due to icy roads.

Brilliant. "Prepare for" and "actual" had far different connotations. He might make the meeting on time. The traffic slowed when he neared the on-ramp. He spotted a city-owned truck dispersing sand and salt on the lanes ahead. In record time, he reached the other side of the bridge. Several minutes later, he pulled into the bank parking lot—only nine minutes late.

A snowplow had shoveled the parking lot of the tinted glass building. He leaped from his vehicle and ran to the entrance. An older woman carrying several boxes blocked the entry as she struggled to juggle her load. Rob raised his arm over her head and pushed the door open.

"Would you mind hurrying a bit, ma'am? I'm late for an important meeting."

The woman readjusted her bundles and turned around. "Young whippersnappers. No patience these days." She thrust the packages at Rob's chest. "Help with these, young man."

He didn't have time for her commands, but his father had taught him to respect older adults. "Where should I place them?" He clutched them while propping the door for her.

The angry woman shuffled into the bank. "Follow me, and don't drop those, or I'll make you pay for them." She led the way to a room past the tellers.

Rob deposited the packages on the table she nodded at before running to the front lobby. Struggling to remain calm, he dashed to the closest teller. "Where's my meeting? Please, I have to sign the paperwork today."

The trim lady behind the plexiglass shield perked up when she saw him. "Dr. Ambrose?"

Rob nodded.

"Mr. Anders buzzed me. He's packing documents as we speak. I'll call him." She pushed a button while Rob chewed the inside of his cheek. "Dr. Ambrose has arrived. He insists on completing the meeting."

Rob raised his hands and whispered, "Which way?"

She gestured to the first door on the left. Rob reached it in a few long strides. He entered without knocking but halted in his tracks. "Please forgive me for barging in. I hope you're not leaving. I'm sure you've experienced bridge hold-ups."

Expressionless, Mr. Anders greeted him. "I'm packed and ready to leave."

"So, I'm too late?"

"A few minutes more, and I would've left the building. You arrived just in time. The buyer signed the paperwork earlier."

Rob released his breath. "How about if I hurry and sign so you can go home?"

In less than sixty minutes, he dashed from the building, happy he'd wrapped up both closings. Smoky clouds blanketed the parking lot as he slid into his car. Snow would begin fluttering any minute. He started the car and asked Siri to buzz Vivi's phone, hoping Sloan would be with her.

No answer.

Did she and Sloan fall asleep from an exhausting day? How could he reach them? Rob needed the phone number for the resort, but he'd left the paperwork in the mansion when collecting his summer clothes for the vacation. A quick trip to his childhood home was in order. He had thirty days to remove all belongings before handing the keys to the buyer.

Twenty minutes later, he entered the mansion, expecting to feel overwhelming sadness for selling it, but the majestic beacon in the community for many generations had become more than he could manage. And living alone in the sprawling estate was unbearable. Recently, he leased an apartment near the hospital and brought one staff member, middle-aged Mrs. Paley, as his live-in housekeeper. With his busy clinical and surgical schedules, he welcomed her handling the household tasks.

He opened the door and walked down the hallway, admiring the expensive artwork. An art-house auction would sell most of the items. He'd use the funds to pay for the Marysville home.

His formal, posh lifestyle would soon dissipate into a less stressful existence. But he worried about not having a waitstaff. Perhaps Sloan would allow Paley to live with them. Paley would appreciate the job.

Upon entering the study, Rob admired the inviting room. Its large windows allowed sunlight to illuminate the paneled walls, and two bookcases showcased his favorite books. The leather furniture would fit well in his new home.

He rifled through the papers on his cluttered desk, searching for the bill from the resort. The desk's open drawer alerted him to its location. A sticky note pasted on a printout for the Las Palmeras lay inside. He recalled the price he'd paid for a seven-day package for himself and two coworkers because they needed the time away from their busy schedules for relaxation.

He found the resort phone number in the bill's header and dialed it on his landline.

A pleasant voice answered, "Las Palmeras, how may I serve you?"

"Rob Ambrose, here. Can you confirm if Sloan and Vivi Evans arrived?"

Silence followed.

"No, sir. They haven't checked in yet."

"Would you please verify it?" Rob sat on the edge of his desk, rubbing his eyes to fight exhaustion. It was unbelievable she and her sister hadn't arrived.

"They haven't registered or picked up their keys. Their check-in time is overdue." The desk clerk spoke firmly this time.

"Right. They should've landed at the airport hours ago. What could have happened to them?"

"You'll have to discuss it with your friends and the airport, sir."

Worry and fatigue eroded Rob's ability to think. He ended the conversation and called Paley. "I haven't heard from Sloan and Vivi. I'm concerned."

Paley responded in her motherly tone, "Stop worrying, Rob. It hasn't been twenty-four hours since they departed. They'll need time to settle."

Stop worrying? How could he do that when he was a natural-born worrier? He paced beside the desk with a hundred thoughts racing through his head. Perhaps he was overreacting, but on the other hand, Sloan's life might be at stake. He handled hospital and cardiac emergencies without panicking. Granted, this was a different matter, but regardless, he had to get a grip.

"Would you like me to get the ticket for a flight in two days?" Mrs. Paley asked.

"Never mind. I'll find a way to get there tonight. I have to make sure Sloan and Vivi are safe."

"I know you'll do what's best, Rob."

He ended the call and searched his address book for friends who knew pilots. Would he find one available on such short notice?

Chapter Seven

S cattered debris surrounded Sloan as she opened her eyes and found herself sprawled on her back. Beyond her foot, waves splashed toward her before retreating and continuing the sequence. It wouldn't be long before the water covered her body. She dug her nails into the earth at her sides and sifted warm sand through her fingers. "Somebody. Help me," she cried.

The world spun and cramps seized her abdomen as she raised her head. She braced her belly to ease the dry heaves, but the lack of saliva on her parched, swollen tongue made spitting anything, especially the grit coating her mouth, impossible. She needed water, but first, she had to stand and find higher ground.

Beyond her foot, a white object billowed on the water. Was it hers? She patted her body and found nothing missing except her leg. *Her leg?* Shrieks sliced the air as adrenaline filled her veins.

Shaking uncontrollably, she raised to her elbows, but piercing pain stabbed her head and sent her reeling to the sand. She clutched her head and tried again, slower this time. Dizziness and rhythmic dry heaves increased as she cupped her eyes against the sun. Nearby, a hazy form with hair draping its shoulders watched her from a hill. Something dark covered the figure's eyes.

Her world went black.

Chapter Eight

An ear-splitting explosion shattered the serenity along the unspoiled shoreline where Jameson and Nicholas planned to surf. The horse drawing their wagon reared on its hind legs before galloping down the beach. Jameson tightened the reins. "Whoa, Blaze, easy now, buddy."

Once the horse came to a stop, Jameson and his brother leaped from the wagon and scrambled up a dune as a plane sank beneath the sea's waves.

"Look, there's a body on the beach. Could be more survivors in the water." Jameson released the binoculars strapped around his neck and raced Nicholas to the lifeless form.

Propeller blades, metal plane parts, shoes, and soggy seat stuffing littered the sand near a woman sprawled on the beach, her arms curled by her head. One foot lay beneath her thigh, the other leg outstretched.

Nicholas dove into the water while Jameson ran to help the woman. Before reaching her, he pulled a scarf from his pocket, positioned it beneath his eyes, and tied it behind his ears. Satisfied it covered his face, he dropped to the sand and placed his ear near the lady's mouth. Minimal air exchange. Taking care, he brushed the sandy hair from her face. Blood that trickled from her nose, left dark smears on her cheek. He wiped away the sand clumps from her neck and searched for a pulse below her jawline. Thready. She was barely alive. But for how long?

Nicholas dove under the water several times, returning to the surface for air when necessary. After futile attempts to locate survivors, he waded to the water's edge and plodded up the beach. "No other bodies." He fell to the sand and sucked air to catch his breath. "But two more seat cushions are missing from the plane. Did you notify Doc yet?"

"That's my plan." Jameson removed a rectangular communication device from his pocket and pushed the button. Static erupted. "Dr. Boyd. Come in, Dr. Boyd."

"What is it, Jameson?"

"There's a body on the beach. Young woman. Barely breathing. Can you meet us at the house?"

"Roger that."

Nicholas rolled to his knees and checked her breathing.

"Careful, brother. See the blood matting her hair? She has a head injury. Keep her neck rigid until we learn whether it's broken." Jameson tucked the Walkie-Talkie in his pocket and ran to the horse-drawn wagon they'd brought. He gathered his surfboard and beach towels before hurrying back to Nicholas. The lightning bolt on his board signified his second chance at life.

He slid it to the sand. "Here, we can roll her on this."

"Great idea." Clad in swimming trunks sans shirt, as was Jameson, Nicholas rubbed the nape of his neck. "Good thing we learned about spinal cord injuries during our military first aid training. Maybe we can save her life."

"We learned a lot about survival, didn't we?" Jameson helped his brother unfold one leg from under her bottom before placing rolled beach towels on each side of her neck. Satisfied they had immobilized her spine, they logrolled her onto the board and avoided jerky movements as they lifted her into the wagon.

"I'll stay with her," Jameson said. He jumped into the back. "Drive the horse with care, Nicholas. I'm counting on her survival."

"Now, Jameson, don't get any ideas. You know nothing about her."

"I can dream, can't I?" As wounded as the woman was, he couldn't help but notice her high cheekbones and heart-shaped face. Cleaned up, she'd be a stunner, and he was a fit single man in his prime.

Nicholas scrambled to the driver's seat and tied his flyaway hair into a neck-hugging ponytail. He tugged the reins and clicked his tongue for the horse to set out.

During the trip to the mansion, Jameson inspected the gash on the woman's posterior head. The laceration covered an egg-sized bump, but dried blood had matted her sand-coated hair and stopped the bleeding. He checked her limbs for bruises and breaks and her fingers for rings. She had a swollen foot but wore no rings. She was a single lady. He smiled at the revelation.

Following Jameson's instructions, Nicholas slowed the horse. The ride to the mansion was much longer than usual, but the lady tolerated the trip with merely an occasional moan. Jameson's decision to hire his brother as his attendant when he purchased the island had been a good one.

Despite their isolation from the world, Jameson required his staff to sign contracts when he hired them. They had agreed to remain on the island until Jameson passed. Their pledges comforted him since he didn't expect to live more than a few years. Yet Dr. Boyd's medical expertise had eased his pain, and he slept some nights—reasons for him to celebrate.

Nicholas tugged the reins when they arrived at the mansion. Dr. August Boyd and the handyman, Herbert Sims, met them in the rear driveway. Before they moved the lady, Dr. Boyd quickly assessed her for a spinal cord injury. Although unconscious, she jerked her hands and feet when he pricked them, and her pupils constricted to his penlight. "I doubt there's a spinal cord injury." He dropped the instrument in his pocket. "But let's transport her on the bodyboard. It'll make the move easier."

Together, they carried her to a main-level bedroom. Matronly Ivy Boyd, the doctor's wife, and good-natured Esther Sims, Herb's wife, had placed folded sheets over the bed linens. Jameson waited outside the room while the two cared for the woman.

More than an hour later, Esther opened the door. "We gave the lady a sponge bath and dressed her in a satin nightgown. She's tucked under the silk comforter and sheets."

"Thanks for your help." Jameson entered the room from the hallway where he'd been waiting.

Ivy scooped the lady's colorful skirt and white top in her arms. "She hasn't stirred, but she is breathing." Carrying the bath supplies, she and Esther left the room.

Dr. Boyd entered, clad in his usual shorts and tee. He tucked his thinning gray hair behind his ears and re-examined the woman. "Her swollen foot is discolored, but I don't feel an obvious break. It's more likely sprained, although it's difficult to say whether there's a hairline fracture without an X-ray. Unfortunately, we don't have diagnostic equipment on the island." He shot Jameson a sideways glance.

The doctor had wanted top-of-the-line equipment brought to Paradise Island, but without electricity, it made no sense to own diagnostic machines.

Dr. Boyd retrieved his penlight from his pocket and shined it in the lady's nose, noting the dried blood in her left nostril. "There is no perceptible deformity. A broken blood vessel might be the blood's source." He eased her head to the left. "Other than her foot, the major injuries are head wounds. She has quite a knot and gash posteriorly." He stroked his bearded chin. "I suggest someone stay with her around the clock. In the meantime, keep the makeshift brace on in case there's a hairline neck fracture. If she convulses, I may need to release pressure on her brain. Please alert me for any seizures, unusual breathing, or vomiting."

"I'll stay now and through the night." Jameson lowered himself to an overstuffed armchair beyond the bed. He would be the first person to speak to her.

Dr. Boyd's brow wrinkled. "Are you sure you're up for that?"

"If she awakens, I'll scoot out the door." Or, rather, he'd step behind the dressing screen and speak with her, careful not to show himself until the right time—a few weeks or months if necessary.

"If you're comfortable with the arrangement, then so be it. You're making progress, Jameson." Dr. Boyd clapped him on the shoulder before leaving the room.

Jameson studied the woman's breathing. Her respirations had improved. They were average, not slow or jagged as expected in severe head trauma. An unmarried woman hadn't graced Briggs mansion for years. He'd been a fool to set rules when he purchased the island and built his home. His injuries, as well as his nerves, had been slow to heal. And although disfiguring, his wounds were less shocking now. He could almost bear seeing his reflection.

Esther Sims had begged him to rehang mirrors after Jameson banned them for five years. He had reluctantly agreed because Esther and Ivy needed them, and their husbands pleaded for him to understand.

"Mirrors are not the enemy, Jameson." Dr. Boyd stood firm in supporting the women. "Your critical thoughts are your worst enemy, not what you see in the mirror. In your grieving mind, you distort the truth."

Perhaps the doctor had been right. Jameson checked the hurricane lamps on the fireplace mantel and the sconces on the walls. He had enough replacement candles and oil for tonight.

As he gazed upon the mystery woman lying in bed, hope lit the dark shadows in his heart. Would this breathtaking young lady choose to live on the island with him? Could she overlook what he'd been through and his...

He didn't dare speak of it and relive the pain. Given time, the young woman might learn to love him as he would love her. But would she leave him if transportation arrived on the island? The whole idea of her loving him seemed ridiculous. Theirs would be the most unlikely romance.

Was it wrong in this century to hope for a woman who lacked vanity and worldly influences? Anger over his circumstances refused to allow his old self to die. He missed his past as an assertive, self-confident man not having to hide on an isolated island. He studied the lady's heart-shaped face, slender frame, and the gentle rising and falling of her chest with each breath. She was exquisite. Beautiful. He hoped, above all else, she'd want to stay.

But did it matter? There was no way off the island.

Chapter Nine

Rob smacked the steering wheel. He'd called everyone he knew and left messages for those unavailable, but so far, he'd had no luck in finding a pilot with a private jet. He was about to call Paley when his cell phone rang. "Hello?"

"Hello, Rob. Dr. Alberetti here. I worked with Gray at the Addington Complex before he sold it and started the Marysville clinic. He might've mentioned me."

"Of course. He asked you to work for us if I'm not mistaken."

"True. I would've accepted the offer, but I had to work closer to home."

"Understandable."

"Your phone message indicated you need a flight to Scarlett Bay. I have a pilot friend with a Cessna jet. He'll fly you there, but he's short on time. Tell him I sent you."

"Will do. I appreciate it."

Dr. Alberetti gave him the phone number and directions to the private airstrip. Rob phoned the pilot as he zipped through St. Anne's congested streets. The pilot agreed to fly him to Scarlett Bay if he arrived at the airstrip within the hour.

Thankful he had a flight, Rob abandoned his plan to head to his apartment and wove through traffic. A couple miles outside the city, he maneuvered around an icy bend and spotted a small hangar on a private road. After parking, he dashed across the lit tarmac. A man in a leather bomber jacket walked down the steps of a private jet. "You must be Rob. Ready to fly to the Caribbean?"

"You bet. Let's get this thing in the air." He handed the pilot his luggage and the agreed-upon sum for the flight.

After obtaining clearance from the airport, Cal maneuvered the aircraft into the air. Rob longed to hear Sloan's sweet voice, cute laugh, and encouraging words. There had to be a simple reason why she hadn't arrived at the Las Palmeras. He'd been lucky to reserve accommodations for seven days since the resort was the newest one on the island. He and his coworkers needed the vacation as a refresher from their unyielding patient loads. Perhaps Sloan and Vivi had checked into the wrong hotel. According to the brochures, resorts were abundant on the island.

"Got a lot on your mind?" the pilot asked.

"More than I can handle," Rob replied. "I don't dare close my eyes."

"Snooze if you'd like. I'm not a talker."

Hours later, the Cessna landed in Scarlett Bay. The pilot unloaded Rob's luggage and offered him a business card.

"Thanks. I'll hang on to this." Rob tucked it in his pocket and scanned the empty tarmac. His journey had just begun.

Chapter Ten

Darkness blanketed Scarlett Bay as Rob entered the air terminal and inspected the surroundings. He wasn't prepared for its primitive nature. Harsh overhead lighting cast eerie shadows over the impoverished place. Despite the unbelievable hour, several people, including cabbies, those manning booths, those mopping floors, and several tourists lounging on vinyl chairs sipping coffee, occupied the premises.

A taxi driver stood on her toes and raised a "Taxi" sign. A broad smile enhanced by rosy lips spread her smooth freckled cheeks. "Need ride?" She wagged her blonde dreadlocks along with her sign, wafting baby powder as she moved.

"I'm trying to find someone who gave two American ladies a ride today around noon," Rob said.

"Might go there." The cabbie pointed to a place across from them.

Rob wheeled his luggage to the domestic booth, where a young woman with a rose in her hair sat on a stool, sipping a beverage. "Can I help you?" she asked.

"Only if you saw two American ladies today."

"Many Americans fly here. You have photo?"

"Sure, one minute." Rob scrolled through his cell phone until he found a picture of Sloan in teal scrubs

FIND ME IN PARADISE

with a purple stethoscope around her neck. "Here. Did you see this lady?"

"Yes. Yes. I see her. She with another lady. They take cement steps over there." She hitched her thumb in the general direction. "You're lucky. I work two shifts today. No replacement. Can't keep good help around here."

Rob tipped her a twenty and dragged his luggage to the steps. He dodged the broken cement chunks until he reached the lower level, where more taxi drivers wielded signs.

"Did you see this lady today?" He passed his cell phone to the drivers, who were eager to help.

The curvy blonde cabbie from the upper level appeared downstairs and waited her turn for the photo. "Why you not show me before? I'm Mac. I drive her and other lady to domestic airport." Mac stood by a rusty blue cab pieced together with multicolor doors and a purple trunk.

Rob paused before asking his follow-up question because he feared learning the answer. "Did these ladies fly?"

"Yes. The one in photo and lady with her."

Weak-kneed from an empty stomach, Rob staggered to the cab, trying not to lose ground. The cabbie opened the rear passenger door in time for him to drop inside.

"I go put luggage in trunk," Mac said, closing his door.

Rob couldn't get Sloan and Vivi's fates out of his head. If they didn't arrive at the resort, did it mean their plane crashed? His worst fear might become a nightmare. "Can you drive me to the airport?"

"Yes. Yes. We go now." The cabbie closed his door, but it flew open. She shoved it again and kicked the door so hard it clicked shut. Before Rob recovered from her deed, his feet fell through a small crater in the floor. The travel brochure hadn't prepared him for the primitive island. It used words like "serene seascapes," "easy-going atmosphere," and "pristine beaches." He'd fallen for the picturesque charm.

Straddling the hole, he clung to his seat in the stuffy taxi, wishing he had air and a gallon water jug. He turned the window crank, but the glass failed to budge more than halfway. Resting his head on it, he longed for the cliched tropical breeze.

The cabbie slid into the driver's seat and started the car. After swerving to avoid a pothole, she glanced at Rob through the rearview mirror. His eyes met hers, but he didn't dare budge because his feet might fall through the hole. Why was she studying him?

The cab sputtered down the road for several miles until it reached a structure with three walls, an open garage door, and an airstrip. "Here we are," Mac announced.

The dimly lit hangar and airstrip didn't appear welcoming this late at night. Rob passed a fifty over the seat to the cabbie, who had already extended her palm. "Thanks for the ride. Would you mind waiting a few more minutes in case I need a ride elsewhere?"

"Sure. But meter running."

Rob nodded at her through the mirror, exited the taxi, and headed toward a light inside the hangar. With any luck, someone might answer his questions. On entering the building, he spotted a beady-eyed man staring down at him from a small plane. The man raised a wrench as though questioning his presence.

Rob climbed the steps and looked inside the cabin. "Sorry to bother you so late, but any chance you saw an American lady with two friends today?" He removed the phone from his pocket and passed him Sloan's picture.

The guy's eyes darted one way and then the other as though worried someone might overhear. "She and other lady flew with Juan Trinidad," he said. "But Trinidad no return."

"Did they reach the Las Palmeras resort?"

"Not sure. Sometimes he visit friends on far side of island. You go tomorrow. Take van."

Rob's watch showed ten minutes before midnight. His head throbbed, and his suit clung to his body. "Is there somewhere to sleep in Scarlett Bay?"

"Everything closed now, except resorts. They fill quick. I'm Clive. There's a bed in room over there for free." He angled his head to a door in the side wall.

"Thanks. I'll take it." Relieved to have a room for the night, Rob walked back to the taxi and stooped to the driver's window. "Can you return in the morning? I'll need a ride to the van."

"No problem. I have room at my place for small fee— only five hundred bucks if you don't mind a toddler." The driver's earnest smile and hopeful eyes begged him to agree, but the fee was too steep.

"Thanks. I'd take you up on it, but Clive offered me a bed here."

Mac's shoulders slumped as she removed his bags from the trunk.

"Here you go." He handed her a crisp twenty. "See you in the morning?"

She nodded. As she and her broken-down taxi rattled down the road, Rob winced at the thought of a door falling off before she returned. He shouldered his travel bag and wheeled the suitcase to the appointed room, relieved he didn't have to search for a hotel this late at night. Sleep sounded good after the rough day he'd had.

He reached the door and turned the knob…

A gasp flew from his mouth.

It wasn't the Chicago Hilton.

A twin mattress hugged the floor under oil and food-stained sheets. But they weren't the worst problem.

Trash littered the floor around the bed, and buzzing flies swarmed the sausage and crust leftovers inside a pizza box. He dodged the wadded wrappers scattered over the floor to reach the nightstand, then he closed the pizza lid. Scanning the tiny room, he noticed a desk fan on a nearby metal chair. He thumbed the "on" switch and stooped so the air could hit him square in the face. Despite the whirring noise, the fan eased the heat and dispersed the unpleasant aromas. But he needed rest.

The emotional stress from worrying about Sloan had left him ready to drop, but his sleeping arrangement provided another obstacle. Sitting up all night in the hard-backed chair might avoid critter attacks, but if he didn't sleep, he'd pass out instead of searching for Sloan and Vivi tomorrow.

A scratching sound snagged his attention. A mouse sniffed the pizza box before jimmying open the top and shimmying inside. The rodent hadn't scurried away when Rob entered the room. Was the varmint used to sharing close quarters?

An irritant itched Rob's arm. A flea, or worse yet, a bedbug? He swatted the spot, then another spot, and another. Unable to keep his eyes open, he spread his shirt on the mattress where he planned to lay and rolled his suit jacket for a pillow.

Tonight, he'd dream about Sloan, food, and pestilence.

Chapter Eleven

Unable to focus, Sloan squinted at her surroundings. Nothing looked familiar. Wind gusts ruffled and snapped curtains over the windows to her left. Beneath her, a pillowy mattress covered in sleek sheets and a shiny comforter embraced her sore bones.

She rolled on her side, but a searing pain exploded in her head. Probing through the hair over her scalp, she located the culprit. A significant bump. Her fingertips brought back dried blood.

Beyond the four-poster bed, blurry outlines had her guessing their identities—a sofa, bookcase, ladder, fireplace, and armchairs?

"I'm glad you're awake."

Where was the speaker? Sloan reared back in bed and clutched the covers to her chin. "Who's there?" She moved her eyes, careful not to engage her aching head. "Where are you?"

"Behind the screen. You're my guest."

She hadn't noticed the hazy black panels near a door. "Show yourself."

"Another time. Your head injury is significant, but I monitored your condition through the night. I'm pleased you're awake."

The man's mellow baritone voice was comforting, yet unsettling. "Where am I?" she asked.

"You're in my home on Paradise Island. A small plane sank in the sea before we found you on the beach. You were unconscious. Do you recall your name?"

Sloan attempted to move. "My head hurts."

"I'm sorry. I'll ask Nicholas to bring medication. But I have one last question. Did a female accompany you?"

Darkness filled Sloan's pulsating head. She grimaced at her distressing situation. A female?

"Please don't tax yourself. Try to rest."

The screen shook as if something had struck it. The panels buckled and the partition plunged. Sloan raised on her elbows, eager to glimpse the mysterious man, but the barrier quickly returned to its previous position.

"Who are you? Tell me," she pleaded. Her voice trembled with desperation.

A hand from behind the screen reached for the doorknob and the door opened. Sloan stretched to see the hazy figure with broad shoulders, narrow waist, and long hair depart from the room.

A light breeze ruffled the curtains, stealing Sloan's attention from the stranger's exit. Words and thoughts failed her. She rested on a pillow and closed her eyes. Who in their right mind would hide behind a screen to speak with her? *Was she safe?*

She peeled back the covers and lowered her right leg. As she pressed down on the wood floor, a scream burst from her mouth. Her foot resembled a huge plum. Now she understood the reason for the throbbing pain.

Gripping the nightstand for balance, she raised on her opposite toes and inspected the scenery through the windows. Fuzzy pinks, greens, tans, and blues dotted the land. A chill ran up her spine as she surveyed the unfamiliar surroundings. She had to escape.

She clutched the bed, then a sofa, an overstuffed chair, and a coffee table as she inched to the fireplace. On its hearth, she found a utensil perfect for use as a cane.

She opened the room's door and glanced down a hallway adorned in subtle blues. Flat objects lined the left wall, and across the hall, a long, narrow table displayed stand-up frames. She arrived at the table using the wall and fireplace poker for assistance. Bracing her body on its edge, she brought a frame close to her eyes. Although her vision was blurry, she made out images in the picture. Several men wore camouflage uniforms and stood before a vehicle. She couldn't help but stare at the tallest man, but dizziness overcame her.

Another step sent her reeling to the floor in darkness.

As Sloan opened her eyes, a man with tawny hair brushed his fingers by her chin. "Here's medicine for you, Miss. If you take this pill with water, it'll ease your pain."

A bloodcurdling scream burst from her mouth.

"Sorry. I didn't mean to scare you."

Shivers coursed through Sloan's spine. Not only had she failed to escape, but strangers had access to her room. And someone had carried her to bed.

"Will you please forgive me?" the man asked.

Ignoring him, she rolled the pill between her fingers, inspecting its color and shape before placing it in her mouth. The medicine was acetaminophen, an over-the-counter pain pill. A memory! *Would more follow?* She swallowed the pill with the water, keeping her facial expressions under control.

The man set the cup on his tray and placed it on an end table before approaching the bed again. "Would you mind if I bandage your foot? It might ease your pain and swelling." His tender demeanor soothed her fear.

"Thank you for helping me." She inhaled deeply and a fresh linen scent toyed with her senses as she removed the covers.

Using gentle movements, the man wrapped an elastic bandage around her foot and ankle and raised her limb on several pillows. "There's much swelling, Miss, but this should help the healing. The doctor doesn't think it's broken."

"Where am I?"

"Paradise Island. It's in the Caribbean. We're wondering where you were heading before the crash."

A dark void appeared when Sloan searched for memories, yet spontaneous information popped out at odd times. "I can't remember. Did you find another female?"

"You recalled Jameson asking about her? That's wonderful. Your short-term memory has improved."

"Who is Jameson?" Sloan touched the bump on her head and winced in pain.

"He's my brother. I'm sorry you're in pain. The medicine should help. We found another lady collapsed on the beach about a quarter of a mile from where you washed ashore. Unfortunately, she has a broken arm, and Dr. Boyd and his wife, Ivy, are treating her in their home."

"Who is the lady? Does she know me?"

The trim young man removed a lavender elastic band from his pocket and swept his thick hair into a neck-hugging ponytail.

Sloan had seen the elastic band somewhere.

Rather than answering her questions, the young man scooped the tray from the end table and walked to the door. Before departing, he turned back. "I'm Nicholas. My job is to take care of your needs."

Sloan appreciated his humble manner, even if he was a stranger. "Can you please tell me why a man speaks to me from behind that screen?" She gestured to the black partition by the door.

"You'll learn soon enough." Nicholas's matter-of-fact tone did nothing to calm her uneasiness.

Was he the mysterious man simply disguising his voice? Something wasn't right about Paradise Island.

Jameson glanced up from his stool at the kitchen island when Nicholas entered the room and set the tray on the quartz counter.

"The young lady is asking about you, brother." Nicholas plucked a few grapes from a bowl. "Why won't you show yourself?" He popped the orbs into his mouth.

"Isn't it obvious? I'll do so when the time is right."

"You have a point there, I suppose."

Jameson moved the grape bowl within his reach. "I'll watch over her tonight to ensure her respirations are normal and she doesn't have seizures."

Nicholas stepped outside and returned, holding a pitcher filled with sun-kissed spearmint tea. He placed it on the island beside his glass. "Good ol' Esther. She made this for us." He poured the warm beverage for himself. "Would you care for some?"

"Sure." Jameson walked to the cupboard and selected a glass. "Nicholas, I don't want to scare our guest. Remember what happened last time? My appearance no longer startles you." He slid the glass to his brother and sat on the stool again.

"I'll never forget what happened. I'm sure you'll do the right thing. You always do." Nicholas poured the tea and passed it to Jameson before sitting across from him. "The survivors who washed ashore are young and beautiful."

"True, brother. But they might not be our type."

"Now you're sounding like me." Nicholas sipped his tea. "The heat has drained me today. I'm going surfing. You coming?"

"Sure, but let's take it slow with the ladies." Jameson walked to the decorative mirror across the room, something he rarely did. He viewed his profile before studying his face. Anger over his situation replaced his thoughts about the women. He'd never be the same again.

Chapter Twelve

Rob awoke and cringed at the itching sensations covering his body. Red bumps dotted his limbs. After scratching until he broke skin, he whisked his suit and shirt off the mattress. One whiff, and he knew what he had to do. Lob them into the waste can.

The remaining clothes in his bag were poor choices considering the laid-back lifestyle in Scarlett Bay. Before zipping his suitcase, he donned a stiff-collared, short-sleeved shirt and white shorts.

Weary from inadequate sleep and unpleasant air, he wheeled his luggage to the hangar and inhaled a deep breath of…oil fumes. He choked and coughed for several seconds. Clive glanced up from his cluttered desk as Rob slapped a hundred-dollar bill on the surface. "Thanks," he said, coughing again before hurrying to the exit.

Outside the structure, Rob sucked in the fresh air. True to her word, Mac sat in her multicolored cab where she'd left him last night. He wheeled his suitcase to her window and lowered his head. "Glad you made it back so soon."

"No problem. Looks like the skeeters got you." Mac ran her eyes over his arms and legs. "Nice polka dots."

"Yeah, they sure do itch. Any place I can get medicine?" He climbed in the back as she stretched across the front to the glove compartment.

She removed a pink bottle and cotton balls and handed them over the seat. "Use this. It'll stop the itch."

"Thanks. Much appreciated."

"No problem. Hungry?"

"No appetite."

She passed a capped coffee and wrapped pastry to him anyway. "Try eating."

He eyed the food as if it might contain mouse droppings, but he hadn't eaten since yesterday's breakfast. "Thanks." He sipped the coffee and released a sigh. "This hits the spot."

Mac gave him a thumbs-up and loaded his luggage. She drove him a mile or two down dirt roads until they reached a gravel lot where several older vans sat beside a run-down building. After stepping from her taxi, she opened Rob's door. "You go inside. Driver take you to Las Palmeras." She unloaded Rob's luggage, and he handed her double the fare for all she'd done for him.

"Good luck, mister." She waved and drove away.

Rob walked into the weathered wood structure, holding his breath for what he might discover inside, but he released a sigh when he looked around. The interior resembled a primitive auto mechanic shop. It featured a dirt floor stacked with spare auto parts and smelled of diesel oil.

Farther inside, Rob found a middle-aged man sitting at a counter. "Excuse me, sir, but are you the driver?" Rob swung his leg over a stool beside him.

"Might be. Who's askin'?" The man said in a hoarse voice. He lifted the tattered racecar cap riding back saddle on his head and itched his scalp.

"Rob Ambrose, Mister…"

The man eyed Rob's dotted arms, then chuckled until his laughter ran dry. "It's Easy Joe." He brought a mug to his lips, swigged the liquid, and wiped his mouth with his hand.

"Well, Mister Joe, can you give me a lift in your van or whatever you drive?"

"Like I said, it's Easy. Joe. Let me finish business, then I'll take you to Mars if it's your destination. Have some coffee." He picked up a paper on the counter and began reading.

A fresh-faced lady on the younger side of eighteen dropped greasy screws into a jar behind the counter before walking to Rob. She raised a clear coffee pot filled with a dark liquid. "You like it loaded?"

"Loaded with what?" Critters scurried through Rob's mind.

She nudged a sugar bowl and milk pitcher before pouring the steaming brew into a mug and setting it by his hand.

Rob grimaced as he sipped the liquid, expecting the worst. But his worries were unfounded. It tasted better than most coffees back home. After doctoring it, he took another sip. "How do you say 'delicious' in Spanish?"

"Delicioso."

Easy Joe folded his paper and swiveled sideways to face Rob. "Are you going to the Las Palmeras?" He guzzled his drink and wiped his mouth again.

"Yes." Rob hadn't mentioned where he was going, so how did the man know? "Have you heard anything about some missing tourists?"

Easy Joe tucked the folded paper in his pocket. "Don't know nothing about no Merican ladies."

Hmm. Rob made a mental note to investigate the driver. "How much do I owe you?" He raised his mug at the young lady.

"No charge, señor."

He placed a twenty on the counter, and the lady's face lit up. "Thank you, señor."

Easy Joe watched Rob's every move from the corner of his eye. Cringing from the steady glare, Rob stood.

"Let's go." The driver pivoted off the stool and tucked his scraggly gray hair under the backward cap. Without asking, he swooped Rob's bags from the floor and carried them outside. "No other fares today. You're lucky." He loaded the luggage in the back of a van.

The solid gunmetal blue vehicle without any rust was in better shape than Mac's old clunker. "How long is the trip?" Rob asked.

"Four hours, but I drive fast."

"Perfect. The faster, the better."

Within a few minutes, Rob regretted those words. Easy Joe came alive behind the wheel. He steered one-handed while jabbering about everything known to man as he sped around cliffs on two wheels. He seemed oblivious to the steep drop down the mountainside. Each time the van navigated a curve, Rob gripped his seat. "Would you mind watching the road?" He slammed his hand against the dashboard.

The driver slapped the steering wheel. "I've memorized every cliff and curve. Watch me drive with my eyes closed."

"No, no, no. I believe you. No proof necessary." Bile rose in Rob's throat. He folded his lips over his chattering teeth, trying not to climb out of his skin.

When Easy Joe finally stopped horsing around, a truck hauling chickens drove around the bend on the one-lane road and met them head-on. Easy Joe stepped on the gas and swerved closer to the precipice. His tires spun and rocks flew over the cliff.

Rob's temples pounded. He had a choice—leap out and risk the chicken truck running him over or stay in the van and hope it didn't dive off the cliff. Considering the drop promised a quicker death, he remained in the vehicle and closed his eyes.

Easy Joe seemed to enjoy the challenge while belting reggae tunes from deep in his lungs.

Thankfully, he could sing.

Chapter Thirteen

Rob shifted away from the passenger window and dropped against the seat. He expected gray hairs to sprout from his temples at any moment. The driver's hair-raising dance with death around the cliff had totaled him. "How much longer to the resort?" he asked.

"Two swigs of a…" Easy Joe stopped talking and squinted at Rob as though sizing him up.

Rob had been a fool to wear designer clothing on a primitive island. Any savvy person would have researched how islanders and tourists dressed in Scarlett Bay before leaving home, but he'd been too eager to impress Sloan.

His chin dropped to his chest until the next pothole jerked him awake. He needed sleep but feared snoring if he dozed. Snoring made him think about Liz. She could snore the hair off a dog's back, but her loss affected him more than he imagined. The moment she inhaled her last breath, he felt as though his soul had been sucked out alongside hers. He couldn't get air. A nurse started oxygen on him and called a code. They treated him for asthma induced by shock.

Liz wasn't supposed to die. Rob expected her to recover as she'd done with the last experimental drug.

But she developed anaphylaxis from the medication, and Rob arrived at her bedside when she inhaled her last breath.

For three years after she passed, he wouldn't look at another woman until Sloan arrived at the clinic. Before long, she became an office celebrity. The patients loved her attention. They asked for her when she wasn't there because she treated them like friends.

He had fallen in love with her while refusing to ever fall in love again. He glanced out the window. Somehow, he'd find her and her sister.

Easy Joe screeched into the Las Palmeras's circular drive and slammed on the brakes. The maneuver served its purpose. It startled Rob from his memories, which had spared him from watching the dangerous mountain roads.

"We're here," Easy Joe announced.

Rob stepped from the vehicle and stretched as the driver removed his luggage, deposited it beside the glass entrance doors, and opened his palm.

Easy Joe hadn't been much of a driver, but Rob didn't want to burn the bridge for his return trip to the airport. "Thanks for the ride." He placed several large bills in the man's hand.

As Easy Joe sped away, Rob studied the picturesque resort. The vast stucco structure, a soft sandy pink, possessed a quaint, easy-going charm with its railed porch along the second-story balcony. The place resembled a hotel Rob had seen in New Orleans.

He collected his luggage and opened the glass door.

A petite man in khaki pants and a wrinkled tropical shirt wheeled a tiered rack toward him. "Ready for check-in?" he asked.

Rob handed the man his luggage. "Lead the way."

The porter placed the bags on his rack and rolled the cart along the bamboo floor, past a recessed ceiling with an enormous crystal chandelier. Sunlight coming through the lobby's massive windows struck the light's prisms, causing them to sparkle.

Fresh pineapple and coconut scents teased Rob's senses. Several people in the same uniforms as the porter carried trays laden with frothy drinks speared with fruit slices.

"You care for drink, sir?" A young woman placed a tray under Rob's nose.

He accepted a tall concoction topped by a plump skewered strawberry and sipped. After licking the foam from his lips, he placed a twenty-dollar bill in the lady's hand. "Ahh. This coconut pineapple drink is delicious."

"Thank you, sir."

Rob's excitement grew as he sipped the drink and followed the porter past potted palms and Schefflera trees. Perhaps Sloan and Vivi were in their cottages or lying on the beach. The porter stopped at the fancy marble check-in desk, and a man wearing the same uniform as the other staff greeted Rob. "Welcome. What is your name, sir?"

"I'm Rob Ambrose. Have Sloan and Vivi Evans arrived?" He braced his weary body on the counter and waited for the clerk to check his computer.

The man shook his head. "They haven't arrived yet. We expected them yesterday."

"Me too." The wind sputtered from Rob's enthusiasm. He'd hoped they were relaxing on the beach, far from phones. "Where else would they be?" He propped his elbows on the counter. "Was their flight delayed? Or did you hear of a plane crash?" Rob didn't plan to limit his ideas, but other alternatives were too frightening to ponder.

The clerk backed away from the counter, his palms raised in surrender. "I–I don't know."

"May I have the keys to my cottage, then?" Rob asked.

The clerk deposited the keycards on the counter, pivoted, and hurried through a doorway behind the desk. Rob's skin prickled at the man's indifference. He pocketed his cards and followed the porter and luggage cart. They passed winter-white sofas and upholstered chairs to an exit leading to several stucco cottages.

Lemon, lime, banana, and papaya trees grew between the quaint pastel abodes. The porter informed Rob the fruit was free for the guests. Rob plucked a banana from a large-leafed tree before stopping with the porter at his bungalow. He dropped a bill in the man's hand after he deposited the luggage. Too tired to explore the cottage, Rob closed the door and walked straight to the bedroom where a fluffy comforter draped a king-sized bed. He dropped on his back and soaked in the soft comfort, wishing he had time for sleep. But he had to find Sloan and Vivi before any harm transpired. By now, they'd been missing for twenty-four hours—enough time for the police to take their disappearance seriously. But the question remained—were they somewhere on Scarlett Bay or floating on plane debris in the sea?

He found a phone book on a desk and flipped through the pages, searching for the police department and private investigators. Several detectives had businesses on the island. He wrote the numbers on a desk pad and called Scarlett Bay law enforcement.

An operator connected him to a sergeant who said, "There aren't any recent plane crashes or unidentified bodies on the island. You'll need to come in and file missing persons reports."

Rob added it to his list as a priority, but first, he had to find a detective. Not given to random decisions, he called the front desk, and a familiar voice answered. "How may I serve you, sir?"

"This is Rob Ambrose. I need to hire a detective who can locate my missing friends. Can you recommend one? I want the best. On second thought, I'd like the best of the best."

"Yes, sir. My cousin Delroy is well-known on the island for his expertise. Do you have a pen?"

"I'm ready."

"His full name is Sigmund Arthur Delroy, but he goes by Delroy." The desk clerk rattled off the phone number.

"Thanks." Rob ended the call and tried the number.

After several rings, a raspy voice answered, "Yellooow, Delroy here."

"Sigmund Delroy, the detective?"

Hollow metal cans hit a hard surface. A shuffling noise made Rob think the man had been sleeping, and when he rose, he knocked empty cans to the floor. "Yes, this is him. I mean me."

"Rob Ambrose here. I need a detective ASAP. My friend and her sister are missing. It's been twenty-four hours. You up for the job?"

"Of course. Of course. Where are you?"

"The Las Palmeras. How fast can you get here?"

"Give me twenty. Meet you in the lobby?"

"Good deal." Rob had enough time to shower and change clothes but needed clothing like the locals wore. He called the desk again. "Is there a resort shop here with casual men's clothing? There is? Great. Could someone bring me an islander outfit every day while I'm here? Oh, and add them to my tab. I'm meeting someone in twenty minutes." He gave the clerk his sizes before ending the call.

Ten minutes later, invigorated from the shower's cold water drumming his face, Rob donned the ensuite's guest robe and opened the cottage door. The clerk had placed a package on the doorstep—casual cargo shorts and a blue V-neck tee. Rob dressed and headed to the lobby, ready for sleuthing, but a thought stopped him. How would he recognize the detective? The man hadn't described himself. He reached the lobby and searched the people sipping tropical drinks while milling about. The women's fancy dresses and the men's designer suits appeared suitable for an important event. Rob glanced at the clothes the clerk had selected, and then at the people's clothing in the lobby. Would the detective dress like a professional or a laid-back islander?

Scanning the crowd for the private eye, he spotted an uptight young couple sitting uncomfortably on a sofa and a middle-aged couple browsing through paperbacks and magazines at a kiosk. An unshaven man with scrambled hair and a tee stretched over a beach-ball belly slouched on a stool in the pub. Rob waved at him, but the man turned his head.

On a hunch, Rob headed to the massive lobby doors. Eager to find the detective, he pushed one open. A rusty Oldsmobile Omega from the '80s braked at the curb. The driver's door creaked, and a man sporting a shiny scalp groaned as he placed a foot on the pavement and dragged himself from the sedan. After unfolding, he stood as tall as a basketball hoop with an extra-wide brim. Huffing to catch his breath, he searched the entrance.

Rob glanced back at the guy sitting in the pub. He hoped he'd made a rash judgment. The "slouch" would be perfect for detective work.

The man outside wheezed as he approached the glass doors, taking Rob by surprise. "Looking to hire a detective?" The man struggled to breathe after speaking but raised an inhaler to his lips.

"I'm Ambrose," Rob stated.

The detective walked inside, and Rob released the door. Calling this man had been a bad idea.

The detective tucked the inhaler into his ratty polyester suit jacket from the '80s, the same era as his car. "Nice to meet you, sir. Delroy, former bodybuilder, ex-police officer, and soon-to-be-retired detective at your service." He inspected Rob's dotted arms.

"Bug bites," Rob stated, like it was a fact he didn't wish to discuss.

Locked in a mutual inspection of physical attributes with the man, Rob studied the detective's wide girth but stopped at his gargantuan feet—size twenty—if Rob had to guess. He extended his palm in a business-like greeting.

"Don't do hands. How about we skip it?" The detective displayed an uneasy grin while waiting for Rob's response.

"Sure." Rob rubbed his neck, wondering if the detective could find Sloan or do any job requiring oxygen. "How about if we go inside and talk business?" He did an about-face and led the way into the lobby. The wait staff met them and asked if they'd care for tropical drinks.

Rob needed a new brain more than a drink. What had he been thinking, asking a local for a referral?

The detective scooped a fancy beverage from a young lady's tray. "Don't mind if I do." He tipped his head at Rob when the lady extended her palm.

Rob pursed his lips but extracted a twenty from his wallet and handed it to the lady. "Is there a restaurant in this place? Perhaps we can talk business over food." He shot Delroy a questioning glance.

"Food? I'm game." Delroy gulped a breath before aiming his thumb at the pub ahead. "The Crested Quail serves mighty fine steaks."

Would the detective live through lunch?

A hostess seated them at a booth away from prying ears, per Rob's request. After the server wrote their orders, Rob laced his fingers on the table. "Do you have any credentials?"

He hoped for a resume, but Delroy reached inside his threadbare jacket, produced three items, and handed them to Rob—a folded first-place certificate for a 1999 body-building competition, a tarnished police badge, and a bank deposit receipt from a 2014 detective job. "These good enough?"

Rob closed his eyes and wiped a hand over his face. "I don't suppose you have any references?" He returned the items to Delroy.

"Can't divulge my clients' names. Besides, I don't need no praise reports."

Rob's knees hit the underside of the table. Ignoring his intuition, which encouraged him to end the partnership, he chose to take a chance on the detective. The man seemed to need the money. "These'll do." Rob began sharing details about Sloan and her sister.

Delroy's breathing slowed, but rather than listening to Rob, he glanced over his shoulder several times while tapping his fingers on the table. For a man who needed information on a case, he didn't appear to pay attention. Perhaps Rob's intuition was correct.

When their food arrived, the detective cut into a ribeye steak as big as Texas, and Rob picked at a broiled swordfish before stirring risotto around his plate.

Delroy pierced a meat chunk and paused his fork while inspecting Rob's food. He aimed his little finger, encircled by an onyx ring, at Rob's plate. "In case you're wondering, I ain't fat."

"Never thought you were." *Did Rob offend the detective when he checked out the man's size on arrival?*

Delroy's chest muscles swelled and flexed under his dark spandex shirt as he placed his utensils on the table, removed his ragged suit jacket, and propped it on the booth's bench. After exposing his muscles, he speared an extra-large meat morsel, curled his prominent bicep, and dropped the piece into his mouth.

The display garnered its intended message. The detective might hold his own with a slew of criminals, if he could catch his breath. Muscles were a massive point in the detective's favor. One thing Rob hadn't doubted from the start was Delroy's girth. The man was as solid as a cinder block. "Are you ready to discuss more business?"

"Fire away, boss." Delroy finished chewing and leaned forward, fingers steepled.

"I've already shared the details about Sloan and Vivi. Wherever they are, I want them found as soon as possible. Are you up for the task? There's no time to dawdle or nap, and I expect sixteen-hour days."

Delroy wiped his finger across a sheepish grin as though Rob had exposed him for sleeping when he'd called earlier. "So, you're the overachiever type?" he asked.

"Maybe, or determined, whichever you'd like. But let's find Sloan."

"Let's, boss? What do you mean?"

"I'm going with you. When we find her. I want to scoop her into my arms and—"

"Let's not get graphic." Delroy chuckled as he gathered his suit jacket and slid across the bench.

Heat shot up Rob's face. "We'd better head out then. No time to waste."

"Wait." Delroy eyed Rob's plate. "You going to leave that?"

"I'm not hungry."

"Mind if they bag it for me?"

A few minutes later, they walked to the lobby with Delroy cradling the to-go bag under his arm. He opened the glass door for Rob and stood aside. "After you, boss.

First stop—police station. And by the way, my fee is one grand per day."

Rob arched an eyebrow at him before stepping through the door. "You'd better be worth it."

Chapter Fourteen

Rob gazed at the lush foliage and vibrant flowers along the bumpy road as the detective's car rattled and bounced over the broken pavement.

Driving in silence, Delroy removed an unwrapped cigar from his suit jacket and rolled it between his thumb and forefinger. Now and then he brought the stogie to his nose, inhaled, and released a jaw-dropping sigh. Rob hoped he was savoring the aroma and not planning to light it. Performing CPR on him without an ambu bag and oxygen might not help.

The detective enjoyed his cigar aroma for a few more miles until he parked in the police station side lot and opened the car door.

Rob clapped the glove compartment to nab Delroy's attention. "Do you have any aspirin in there?" He massaged his aching temples from the bumpy ride.

The detective closed the door and reached into his pocket. He lowered his elbow to the window ledge and tossed Rob a plastic bottle with his cigar-wielding hand. "It's not aspirin, but help yourself."

Rob swallowed two acetaminophen tablets without water and set the bottle on the console. "Thanks. These'll do."

"Nurse your pain or come inside. It's up to you."

"Right." Rob lifted the lock button on the timeworn car.

Delroy opened the rusted front passenger door for him, copping a secret service stance. Leaning into a swagger, he led Rob into the police station to an office.

A uniformed officer glanced up from his desk, wielding a half-eaten meat stick like a cigarette as they approached. "Hey, Delroy, you back so soon?"

"Not to stay, Sarge. Got questions about two missing ladies." Delroy tucked the cigar in his suit jacket before dropping sidesaddle on the corner of Sarge's desk.

Following the detective's lead, Rob planted his bottom on the chair beside him.

"How long since they disappeared?" Sarge set aside his coffee mug and placed what remained of his beef stick beside a half-eaten cake slice on a napkin.

"Over twenty-four hours. The two hopped a small plane to the Las Palmeras resort. One lady is Sloan Evans. The other is her sister, Vivi. They didn't check into the resort." Delroy regurgitated every word Rob told him at the Crested Quail.

The sergeant picked up a paper on his desk. "Nope, nope, don't see no missing persons here."

Rob craned his neck to inspect the list. "Your paper is blank."

Sarge leaned his chair back on two legs and yawned. "We don't have crimes involving missing or dead bodies on this small island. I'd wager there's a good explanation for why the ladies haven't checked in." He hovered a pen over his paper. "Give me the details anyway."

"Both ladies have dark-brown hair and a dimple on their right cheek. They're several years apart in age. Departed by puddle jumper from the domestic airport yesterday but didn't make it to the resort. No communications." Delroy glanced at Rob for confirmation when he finished.

Rob nodded at him. The detective hadn't forgotten one word he shared at the restaurant. So he had been paying attention. Perhaps when he looked around while Rob was talking, he'd been scouting for suspects. Rob had no clue how detectives worked. His busy schedule at the clinic and the hospital never allowed him much time for crime shows.

"Any more info?" The sergeant brushed crumbs from his shirt.

Rob pinched the bridge of his nose, trying to siphon information from his tired brain. "I visited the small airport and spoke to a mechanic named Clive. He hasn't heard from Trinidad but says the pilot visits friends on the far side of the island."

The sarge straightened in his chair as though the info had become interesting. "We all know Juan Trinidad. He's a con artist if there ever was one. Laziest son of a sand shark ever to return to Scarlett Bay."

"Return?" Rob raised an eyebrow.

"Left here to attend Harvard. Not sure how he received a diploma. Might have scammed the law professors. Flunked the bar exam several times. He returned several months ago. Now he flies tourists to the island and resorts." The sergeant's words held contempt.

"Sounds like you don't like him." The pilot had flown Sloan and Vivi. Fear gripped Rob, setting his nerves on fire.

Delroy furrowed his brow. "Trinidad is a cheat. He'd rather trick someone out of money than work for it. He was smart enough to land a full scholarship to Harvard, but they almost expelled him for running a betting scam from his dorm room. He talked his way out of that arrest. He's a brilliant idiot, if you know what I mean." Delroy glanced at the sergeant. "We all know him around here. Don't we, Phil?"

The sergeant nodded enthusiastically. "Yup. Only thing is, the islanders are too poor to buy into his petty schemes. It keeps him under control most of the time."

Rob's concerns for Sloan and Vivi's safety boiled over. He jumped up from his seat, unable to contain his emotions for another second. "How soon can the police search begin for Sloan and her sister?"

"I'll contact the Marine division in Jamaica. They'll handle the search and rescue mission. My department will put out an APB and post photos on TV and around the island. I'll need a few if you have them. We'll also ask for volunteers to scour the island." The sergeant reread the details he wrote on the paper. "There's usually a logical explanation when people go missing. Our cell towers provide lousy service. Trinidad might have made an emergency landing on an island, and they haven't been able to call."

"Or, if the plane crashed, they might be floating in the sea. The sooner they're found, the better their chances for survival." Remaining calm during surgical emergencies had become second nature for Rob, but worrying about Sloan? Panic snuffed his serenity. There was no time to waste.

"I'm with you. Let's get the paperwork done." Sarge obtained the information and lifted the phone receiver on his landline. "I'll call Jamaica and let you know when we learn anything."

"I'll be waiting." Rob raised his chin at the doorway for Delroy to leave.

"Thanks for your help, Sarge." The detective removed the car keys from his pocket on their way from the office.

Inside the Oldsmobile, Rob choked down the bitter acid burning his throat. "How about heading to the domestic airport? I'm betting the mechanic knows more than he told me."

"I was going to suggest that. Sarge will send police over there soon. If we get there first, we can interrogate the mechanic before he gets rattled."

"One way or the other, Clive's going to get rattled because I'm not leaving the airport without information about Trinidad." Rob rolled down his window and rested his arm on the ledge. "How long does it take to get there from here?"

"Not too long." Delroy removed the cigar from his inner suit jacket and rolled it under his nose. He closed his eyes for a brief second as he inhaled the aroma. "Mmm."

Rob tried calling the Scarlett Bay airport using a number he'd obtained from the phone book at the resort. Despite repeated calls, no one answered. Thoughts about Sloan ran through his mind during the drive. One and a half days seemed like an eternity since he'd seen the sparkle in her eyes.

When he married Liz, he'd been all business, which fit her personality. They understood each other. Not surprisingly, a few days after she died, it felt as though an earthquake had cracked open the sidewalk, and he'd fallen in alongside her. Three long years passed before he met Sloan, the most caring female he'd ever met. No one would ever take Liz's place, but Sloan enhanced his life in ways he never imagined. She cut through his serious doctor demeanor and returned him to a time when he and his pals used to joke around. Because of her, he began talking from his heart, not from his proper medical or social standing, and it changed his attitude toward patients. He began treating them like friends instead of appointments.

The plush tropical greenery soon changed to huts and shacks as Delroy sped over the dirt road. Many people in Scarlett Bay lived a far simpler lifestyle than those in

American cities. He envied their slow pace and lack of materialism.

When the detective reached the airport, Rob waited for him to uncoil from his car before they headed to the hangar. Clive appeared at the entrance, outfitted in his faded, oil-stained jumpsuit. He eyed Rob and Delroy as they approached.

"Didn't you sleep here last night?" The mechanic raised an oily rag at Rob.

"Yes, thank you, but I have a few more questions. Have you seen Juan Trinidad?" Rob asked.

"His plane crashed. A fishing boat captain found him floating in the sea. Brought him here today." Clive glanced at the closed room where Rob stayed the night. "He's sleeping."

Rob's knees buckled at the word crash. So it was true. Delroy led him to Clive's desk chair and plunked Rob in the seat.

"Say, you got any water?" Delroy gestured to the mechanic.

Clive rose from his desk and filled a paper cup from a water cooler. "Here, this'll do." He ran the cup to Delroy.

Delroy snatched it and threw the cold contents in Rob's face.

Rob bolted upright. "Why'd you do that? My eyes were open." Using his T-shirt, he wiped away the dripping water.

Delroy shrugged. "I need you alert, boss. Wake Trinidad for us, Clive."

Clive stepped between the detective and the door and crossed his arms. "Not a good idea. Trinidad needs sleep."

"Well, ain't you admirable—worrying about his shut-eye." Delroy straightened to his full, towering height.

"Hate to break it to you, Clive, but he ain't gettin' no sleep until we learn why he's here and the ladies aren't."

Clive peered up at Delroy's drawn face and knocked on the door several times before twisting the knob. When it failed to open, Delroy pounded on it and shouted in a police officer's voice, "Open up!" He waited a few seconds before kicking the door open.

The mechanic leaped past Delroy into the room and shook the ginger-haired man curled on the mattress. "Hey, two guys wanna talk to you. Something about those women." Clive glanced at Delroy and Rob before dodging them on his way out the door.

Delroy entered the room with Rob close on his heels.

Glassy-eyed with seaweed gnarling his hair, Trinidad pushed upright to the bed's edge. "Sorry. Plane have engine troubles. No see ladies after crash."

"Cut the B.S., Trinidad. The police told us you graduated from Harvard, so talk like an educated man." Rob had no patience for Trinidad's act. "How is it a boat rescued you but didn't save Sloan and Vivi? Did the captain search for them? Weren't you concerned for their safety?"

"I wasn't right in my head. Sea birds were pecking at it. When the boat sailed by, the captain saw the flock and found me floating over a seat cushion." Trinidad coiled on the mattress. "I need sleep."

"You need to answer my boss's questions." Delroy pulled Trinidad up by the scruff of his wrinkled tropical shirt. "You'd better answer."

The pilot shoved his palms at Delroy. "Wait, wait, wait!"

Blasting forced air through his clenched teeth, the detective opened his fists, and Trinidad landed on the mattress in a crumpled heap.

"I'm telling the truth. I don't know where the plane went down or what happened to the women." Trinidad

raised on his elbows. "We were in the air one minute, and the next, we hit the water. That's all I recall."

Rob didn't believe a single word. "The boat captain ought to know where he rescued you. We need the coordinates."

"But my plane went off course. There's no telling how long I floated in the sea." Trinidad collapsed on the bed and pulled the pizza-stained sheet over his head. "Let me sleep."

"Cough up the captain's name, and we'll leave." Delroy hovered over him, his biceps swelling under his suit jacket.

"Forget him, Detective. I have a better plan." Rob turned on his heels to the hangar, Delroy close behind, and found Clive working on the plane. "Do you remember who rescued Trinidad?" Rob said.

Clive descended the cabin's steps and rifled through the cluttered desk until he found a bound address book. "Captain Reynauld." He tore the page and slapped it on the desk. "Now, let me work. This plane needs repair by tonight."

"How about the address where Trinidad stays after a flight?" Rob asked.

"How would I know?"

Delroy eyed Clive as though the man hadn't given up all he knew, but the mechanic clenched his jaw and fists before returning to the plane.

"Let's see what the captain has to say." Rob removed the cell phone from his cargo shorts and called the number.

A man answered on the first ring. "Captain Reynauld, how may I help you?"

"Rob Ambrose here. Juan Trinidad's plane crashed in the sea with my friend and her sister on board yesterday. He says you rescued him. Did you search for the ladies too?"

"I'm sorry. I saw Trinidad but no other survivors."

"No survivors?" The words sucked the air from Rob. Should he believe the captain? Did he really search for the others? "Will you tell us the coordinates where you found Trinidad?"

"I would if I could, but my compass wasn't working. I'd guess Trinidad was roughly sixty miles south of the Scarlett Bay coastline."

A broken compass on the very day Trinidad's plane crashed? Rob sensed something was amiss, but confronting the man wouldn't be wise if they had more questions. "At least it's a clue. Thank you for your time," Rob said before ending the call.

Delroy must have noticed his defeated expression. "Look, boss, I'll notify Sarge about what we've learned, and we can head back to my office. It'll help the search and rescue team."

"Good. Let's not waste time."

Delroy drove them to a dilapidated shack behind a seedy motel. On the inside, the place had a desk and a scrappy wooden table topped with papers, folders, and overlapping mug rings. Charts, police reports, and photos covered the walls, and a bright light hung from the ceiling.

"Excuse the mess." Delroy swiped scattered papers aside on the table. "I haven't gotten around to cleaning."

"No problem. Do you have a significant other?" Delroy's office suggested bachelorhood.

"Had one," the detective replied. "After I left the police department, she gave up on me."

"Why?"

"I got too wrapped up in my cases," the detective said, removing a pointer stick from his desk. "My girlfriend wanted me home, but I had to earn a living." He walked to the far wall and pulled down a chart. "These are the Caribbean islands."

Rob noticed a plaque with a fish outline on Delroy's desk. It contained the letters—IXOYE. Rob's doctor friend, Ethan, had a similar plaque on his clinic desk, but Rob had no idea what it meant. He joined the detective at the chart. "I didn't realize there were so many islands."

"There's over seven thousand in the Caribbean, boss. Searching each one would be impossible. The stakes are mighty steep for finding the ladies." The detective rubbed his hairless dome. "It would be like trying to scuba dive for tiny diamonds in the sea. If the ladies drowned, we'll never find them. Certain fish will use them for food. But searching the islands will be risky too. Some are dangerous—inhabited by wild animals, or worse yet, wild humans—druggies, illegal cargo smugglers, and human traffickers."

Rob's heart dove. Horrible things could have happened to Sloan and Vivi. He swallowed a sickening lump in his throat before replying, "I'm not giving up. Considering what we're facing, I think we'd better start early tomorrow morning because the only thing setting the stakes for me is my love for Sloan."

"Fine, boss. I'll pick you up at ten."

"Make it nine."

Chapter Fifteen

Sloan awoke as the first sunrays streamed through her windows. Drawn by the gentle rush of waves spilling over the shore, she rose to her knees, and the beach met her gaze. She longed for the outdoors.

She raised her gown and inspected her foot. The swelling had diminished, but the plum-colored bruising persisted. Nicholas's care had helped. Was he the physician, a staff member, or did he own the mansion?

A shadowy figure from her memories came to mind. "Take slow...deep...breaths." The man's warmth and soothing words comforted her, but his face was unclear.

She glanced down at her lace-trimmed nightgown. The housekeeper had set it out last night but hadn't provided day clothes for this morning. Sloan needed a plan. She moved to the bedside as a citrus scent filled the room.

"Good morning, Miss."

Sloan swung her legs under the covers and pulled the comforter to her chest. Her gaze darted around the room, searching in vain for the speaker. "Where are you?"

"Behind the screen. It's best for now." The steady voice urged her to understand.

"Best for whom?" Sloan said. Moving the screen and exposing the man wouldn't take much effort. But what would happen if she tried?

As if he'd heard her thoughts, the man spoke. "My appearance might frighten you. I can't take a chance on you finding me monstrous."

Monstrous? Questions multiplied faster than answers. Why would his appearance scare her? What were his intentions? Why all the secrecy?

"I'm here to inform you that the other lady is safe and comfortable. Nicholas told me you inquired," Jameson said.

"Do you have new clues about our identities? Or why we washed ashore?"

Would the man see her if she tiptoed close and peeked around the partition? She scanned the room for the fireplace poker. It was nowhere in sight. Limping without it wouldn't be easy.

"Nicholas and I witnessed a small plane sink under the waves, but the details eluded us."

"Maybe the woman knows what happened. Would you take me to visit her?"

"Your healing must come first."

Sloan's stomach cramped, and she doubled over in pain. Relax. Breathe. "Will you at least tell me about yourself? Your name? Anything?" *What did the man mean about looking monstrous?* She scanned the room for something she could use as a weapon to defend herself. There was nothing nearby but a book. She'd lob it at his head if need be.

"I'm Jameson Briggs. I own this island, and Nicholas is my younger brother by six years. We have four staff members who live simple yet comfortable lives."

"Judging by the furnishings in this room, you're wealthy."

"Our parents owned Briggs Pharmaceuticals, the largest drug company in the world. When they died, I inherited their fortune and the company. It continues to yield profits. But they won't affect us on this island. I won't bore you with facts and figures, Miss."

"Your story doesn't bore me at all. I'm bored because you've confined me to this room. It's beautiful, but I'd prefer sunbathing, swimming, or anything outdoors. And I'd like a companion for conversation."

"But Dr. Boyd says your brain must rest to heal. We shouldn't allow anything to stimulate it."

"Dr. Boyd? Who is he?"

"He's a retired doctor who lives a quarter mile up the beach. You'll meet him when you can travel."

The reassuring voice answered one question, but Sloan had more. "Have you notified the police about the plane crash or the survivors?"

"Not yet. As I said, we're allowing you time to heal."

"But I'm feeling better, and I'd like the police to post a picture in case people are worried about me."

"Calm down, Miss. The doctor insists for you to take it easy. Brain surgery would be most difficult on this island, but I assure you, Dr. Boyd has prepared for any problems."

"I want out of here!" Sloan threw off her covers. "Please fly me to a hospital." She swung her legs over the bed's edge. "I beg you, please, take me there. Alert the police."

"Return to bed, or I'll have to call Nicholas for help."

The man could see her. Sloan slipped her legs under the covers.

"In answer to your requests—I'm afraid those options aren't available. We have no technology or means for travel. I prefer isolation."

Why would he avoid technology and travel? Was he a lunatic? Something wasn't right. "The least you can do is show yourself."

"I will in time. Yesterday, you passed out on the hallway floor, holding a photo. I placed the picture on the mantel over your fireplace."

Sloan turned to the mantel and spotted the distressed wood frame. In the picture, four men in military fatigues stood before a vehicle—a tank. "Who're the men in the picture?"

"My Marine buddies and I. I'm the tallest."

Sloan swallowed. He was the most handsome man in the group, so something dreadful must have happened to him after someone took the photo.

A knock struck the door, and Nicholas entered, bearing a tray. "Good morning, Miss."

"It's not a good morning. Please, take me to a hospital and tell the police to search for my identity."

Nicholas placed a serving platter on her lap— poached eggs, thick slices of bread slathered with strawberry jam, red juice, and a mug filled with coffee. "You'll feel better after you eat." He opened his palm, which held a pill. "This will help. It'll reduce your pain and swelling."

"I don't want it."

"It's for your good. Since leaving the island is impossible, Dr. Boyd ordered this medicine for your healing."

"Will it make me sleepy?"

"It will decrease brain swelling, which might be the cause of your paranoia." Nicholas moved his palm closer.

"If I'm paranoid, it's from the four walls of this room. I hate being a prisoner!" Sloan swiped the pill from his hand. It was dexamethasone. She'd had patients on the drug. Where had the recollection come from? Was she a medical provider? She'd keep the info tucked away until more memories surfaced. "Nicholas, at least tell me about your brother."

"No more questions!" The man behind the screen slipped through the door, showing his backside.

Sloan's vision wasn't as fuzzy now, and she observed thick tawny hair draped around broad shoulders and a trim torso that tapered to the waist.

Nicholas cleared his throat.

Had he caught her staring?

"You'll learn more concerning my brother soon. Jameson wishes the best for you."

So Nicholas wasn't the man behind the screen, but he had a possible lunatic for a brother? *Could she trust Nicholas?* More than that, she wanted to know more about Jameson's monstrous appearance.

Jameson walked to the kitchen and paced before the stone fireplace. Had he shared more than he should? Would the lady think him crazy? The details about his parents were true, as were his profession and the picture of him standing beside his buddies. So far, so good. He hadn't lied—at least not yet. How much longer until it became necessary?

Esther Sims, his cook, set a metal pot on the wood-burning stove. "If I'm not mistaken, you're in a better mood today, Jameson."

"We'll see," he replied.

"Have you told the lady your story?"

"A little bit, but I don't want to scare her."

"She'll understand after you reveal yourself."

Jameson groaned because his staff imagined everyone wanted the best for him as they did. "Esther, you know the gal might freak out."

"All I know is you can't forge a relationship until you deal with your fears and move on. If the lady likes you, it'll be for who you are, not for superficial things. Veronica desired what you possessed. After your discharge from the hospital, she treated you like you'd lost everything. She wasn't the one for you. The lady who admires you for who you are and values your accomplishments is a keeper. I suppose it's necessary to discuss your wealth, but not this early in a relationship."

Her advice came too late. His inheritance had slipped out because he feared losing the woman. Veronica had refused to live on the island after she arrived. She wanted to see the world. Had she used his injuries as the perfect excuse? Or was he, indeed, a monster as she'd called him?

He let out a moan and clutched his abdomen. "The pain has returned."

Esther gripped his arm and led him to a stool at the kitchen island. "I'll fetch the doctor straight away."

"Hurry."

Chapter Sixteen

Clad in the same ratty suit from the day before, Delroy parked by the Las Palmeras entrance at 9 a.m. Lacking a new set of island wear, Rob had also donned the same clothes from yesterday. He hoped the desk clerk would drop off new clothes before the day ended. Sparing the detective from exiting his car, Rob bent down to the passenger window.

Delroy stretched across the seat and unlocked the door. "Morning, boss."

"I have something for you." Rob tossed him a wrapped Danish from the lobby.

Delroy bit into the creamy cheese pastry and lifted his eyes to heaven. "Umm, got any more of these?"

Rob opened the door and slid into the passenger seat. "Perhaps we can grab lunch later."

"Long as you're buyin', I'm good," Delroy said as he polished off the pastry and licked his fingers. "I'd rather not change the subject when discussing good food, but we should head back to the domestic airport. Trinidad might remember more today. Besides, we can study the airport's flight maps and decide on a plan." The detective pulled the cigar from his pocket and passed it under his nose before adjusting the rearview mirror and shifting into drive. "I love the smell of good tobacco."

"Your lungs thank you for not smoking." Rob hoped Delroy wouldn't give in to temptation. Given his huffing and puffing, while he was speaking, his lungs wouldn't handle it. "I doubt Trinidad will give up more information. But are the maps any better than yours? We could waste valuable time." Rob braced his arm on the window ledge, prepared for another bumpy ride.

"They pinpoint strategic islands. I use them to find drug smugglers and other criminals." Delroy placed the cigar under his nose as he steered away from the resort.

"Did you catch any—criminals?" Rob asked.

"Pirates are my spec-i-al-ity. They can't hide from old Delroy."

Rob's dismal mood improved at the detective's mention of catching criminals, even if he did mispronounce specialty. Tiny diamonds and drugs would be hard to find in the vast Caribbean, but Delroy had a propensity for locating them, if that's what Rob understood. "I've been thinking about the stakes you mentioned, Detective. They don't matter. I need to learn what happened to Sloan and Vivi, even if it means spending everything in my savings account."

"Don't say that out loud around here, boss."

Rob caught Delroy's drift. The islanders seemed to bleed tourists of money. His eyes panned the rut-infested road. "Might want to avoid the craters this time and give my head a rest."

Delroy eased off the pedal and maneuvered the vehicle carefully, unlike the day before. A few miles down the road, he turned and braked at the small-scale airport. Clive stood outside the hangar, wiping his hands on an oily cloth. After Delroy parked, he lowered his head to Rob's window. "Trinidad not here. Had business at main airport."

Delroy stepped from the car and glared down at the mechanic like a gangster calling out a rat. "We'd like to see your flight maps. Mind if we have a look?"

"If you'll let me get my work done afterward, follow me." Clive turned on his heels and walked back to the hangar.

The detective cast a knowing glance at Rob before tailing the mechanic into the building. Rob double-stepped to keep up with Delroy's lengthy strides. "Do you think Trinidad's here?" he whispered.

"I'd bet on it. But us fighting two men might not fare well for you, boss."

Rob rubbed his fist. "I've never punched anyone."

"Exactly. I could take out one at a time, but the other guy might clobber you while I'm at it."

Inside the hangar, Clive walked behind his desk and plucked a rolled chart from a canister. He spread it over a barrel top wide enough to double as a table. "This here's Trinidad's route."

Delroy hovered over the chart. "You got a pencil, Clive? Trace the route for us, and we'll track the islands along the way."

Clive grimaced, snatched a pen and pencil from his desk, and returned to the barrel in a huff. "Many things alter routes—high winds, too many birds..." He drew a faint line from the airport to the Las Palmeras with the pencil, then gave the detective the pen.

Rob removed the scrap paper from his pocket and borrowed the pencil to copy the coordinates.

The detective's jaw tightened. "Uh, boss, I don't subtract a cent if you do my job." He slapped his notepad against his palm.

"Don't worry. You'll get your money. We'll have a good start here." Rob thumped the paper in his hand and tucked the pencil behind his ear. "Ready to head out whenever you are."

"I'll call the police department and give them the information. Maybe they have news for us." Delroy removed an old cellular phone from his pocket. He poked numbers before placing it to his ear. "Yellooow, Lieutenant. Delroy here. Got any news about the missing ladies...No? I see...Got some coordinates for you—Trinidad's usual flight pattern to Las Palmeras." Delroy shared the information and ended the call. "No news. Seems Trinidad hasn't reported the plane crash."

"Why not?"

"He'll lose his license. A police detective learned his plane is missing doors. If the ladies aren't found, he could face homicide charges, too." Delroy scribbled something on the notepad before glancing at Clive.

The jumpy mechanic scanned the hangar again.

"I want Trinidad found for more questioning." Rob's jaw tensed as Clive began fumbling through his desk drawers.

"He's likely hiding in case the ladies' bodies have washed ashore somewhere, but they'd become shark food before making it to land." Delroy tapped Clive's pen on the table to produce more ink. "You got a better writing tool, boss?"

Rob's gut knotted when he handed the detective the pencil from behind his ear. He saw black as he leaned on the makeshift table.

"You okay?"

"Too much talk about shark food and ladies' bodies." Rob looked for a chair, but Clive occupied the one at his desk.

Imagining Sloan at the bottom of the sea was more than Rob could handle. With his back against the barrel, he eased down to his knees.

Clive huffed over to Rob and shoved a coffee mug under his nose. "I don't have time for this."

Rob accepted the drink and gulped the liquid. His face writhed from the horrific flavor—mud—cold, day-old mud. Not that he knew what mud tasted like, but if he did, this would be it. "Mind if we focus on finding Sloan and Vivi alive?" he asked Delroy. Despite the vile taste, the caffeinated brew jolted him to life. He inched to his feet and handed Clive the mug. "Thanks, I guess."

"How about we head to sea, boss?" Delroy jotted something on his notepad and placed the pencil on Clive's desk.

"You own a boat?"

"Do sharks swim in the sea?" Delroy replied.

"Right. Let's get you lunch first and make it quick."

Chapter Seventeen

The detective's sedan rolled to a stop in the parking lot of a seedy café. The place resembled a dive near St. Anne's inner-city free clinic where Rob and the owners of the Marysville clinic, Doctors Gray and Saige Addington sometimes volunteered at Christmas.

Rob shielded his eyes from the sun as he sized up the debris surrounding the place. "Is this café safe?" He hesitated before walking to the door.

"You'll be okay. I'm here." Delroy pursed his lips and whistled a shallow breath. Swaggering like a nightclub bouncer, he opened the door and headed into the joint.

Rob hoped Delroy was as capable as he claimed. He entered the dimly lit establishment behind the detective. "Is this dusky lighting normal?"

"Saves on electricity." Delroy sidled up to the counter and planted his bottom on a stool.

An older, sinewy man walked through the swinging kitchen doors behind the counter. "What can I do you for, Detective?"

Delroy aimed his thumb at the man and glanced at Rob. "Boss, this here's Kingfish. He and Little Mama own the place."

Kingfish raised his hat in greeting, uncovering a shiny head. A gold looped earring dangled from his earlobe.

After introductions, Rob roosted on a stool beside the detective. A framed young Dolly Parton picture, circa big hairdo, hung cockeyed on one side of the room, and a Willie Nelson picture with a braid hanging behind his shoulder occupied the opposite wall. A few busted chairs rested against a wall.

"We'll take two iced colas to start." Delroy opened a menu lying on the counter.

Kingfish flipped a switch, and the lights came on. He collected two glass-bottled colas from a red cooler before using his hand to pop the tops off on the counter's edge. Deed accomplished, he passed them to Rob and Delroy.

"What'll you two have to eat?" Kingfish moved a toothpick up and down between his teeth as he spoke out the side of his mouth. An anaconda tattoo slithered up one arm and a cobra tattoo prepared to strike from the other forearm.

"I'll take a burger with the works." Delroy closed the menu and glanced at Rob. "What about you, boss?"

Rob eyed the hissing snake. "Any risotto on the menu?"

"I can toss a cheese slice over some instant rice." Kingfish winked at Rob.

Rob refused to smile at the cook's attempt at humor. "Never mind. I'll have a well-done burger minus the toppings."

Kingfish collected two frozen burger patties from a freezer and slapped them on the grill. A few flips later, he shuffled them on fried buns and passed a fully loaded burger to Delroy and a plain one to Rob.

Food was the last thing on Rob's mind. The burger didn't taste bad, but he pushed the plate aside after a few bites. "How many islands do you think we can visit in one afternoon?" he asked Delroy.

"What's wrong, boss? Isn't that the best burger you've ever eaten?"

"Might be if I had an appetite. Did you hear my question, Detective?"

"Yes, boss. It depends on whether there are inhabitants on the islands. If we see nothing on the coast, we'll move along, but if we're suspicious, we'll go ashore and investigate."

Kingfish stood nearby, his head angled at Rob and Delroy. He removed a cigarette pack from his rolled T-shirt sleeve when the detective looked his way. "Mind if I smoke?"

Delroy's longing for tobacco surfaced on his sad-sack face. "Help yourself. I'd be smoking too, if I hadn't been forced to quit." He removed the cigar from his jacket, rolled it under his nose, and sighed. "We're in a hurry anyway. Hand him the bill." He gestured with an upturned jaw at Rob, who removed his wallet and withdrew money.

The middle-aged cook eyed Rob as he counted four bills totaling twenty dollars and placed them on the counter. "Keep the Change."

"You're mighty kind to leave me a couple o' quarters." Kingfish removed the toothpick and crossed his arms over his chest. He sucked the back of his teeth, making a tsking sound.

"Sorry." Rob rummaged through his wallet for another twenty. The islanders he'd met were money-hungry. Rob recalled Easy Joe and Mac's behavior while removing cash and placing it on the counter.

"Now, we're talking." Kingfish scooped up the forty dollars and tucked the bills in the cash register. "You want that burger to go?"

Rob nodded but hoped he didn't have to pay another twenty-dollar charge for the bag. The cook wrapped the burger and handed him the sack. Smoke billowed behind the swinging kitchen doors. "Is there a fire back there, Kingfish?" Rob jumped up and turned, prepared for a quick exit.

"Not to worry. It's my old lady's cooking. She's half deaf and don't hear the timer. Meat gets charred, but the smoke clears."

Rob stared at the detective's plate as a hint to finish eating. "You ready to go, Delroy?" Sitting on their bums wasted daylight hours, and Rob wanted to check as many islands as possible.

Lifting his burger remnant, the detective asked, "Hey, Kingfish, any word on the streets about two missing American tourists?" He polished off the last morsel.

"Nope. Ain't heard nothing 'bout no missing ladies, but I'll keep my ears open."

"Thanks. I'll check back later." Delroy retrieved his cigar from the counter and passed it under his nose for one last whiff. "Ready?" he asked Rob before tucking the cigar in his jacket.

Rob beat the detective to the door. "Is Kingfish trustworthy?" He and Delroy hurried from the café without turning back. The way the cook bored a hole in Rob's wallet had made him uneasy, just as Easy Joe had made him wince during their drive around the mountain.

"Not really. I think you've been right all along. Something's going on. I never said, 'ladies.' He has information, but we can't push islanders too hard. They have a network. We need to chill until there's more to go on." Delroy opened his car door and planted his hand on the roof for an assist inside. "Oh, and before I forget—I told you before, don't count money in front of nobody. They'll up your prices." He started the sedan and stepped on the gas.

"I forgot." Rob studied the paved road dotted by lofty homes with massive windows until the view shifted to shacks and lean-tos.

Delroy swerved into a marina and exited his car. Rob followed him on a path that crooked around to prominent docks surrounded by immense boats. He inspected each yacht, his mind ablaze as to which vessel belonged to the detective. Delroy had to be swimming in cash, his office and clothes merely decoys to convince Rob he was poor.

The detective continued walking past the enormous yachts, cabin cruisers, and speedboats until they arrived at a section where they docked smaller boats. "This one's mine." He aimed his thumb at an old, creaky cruiser.

Its shabby seats and steering wheel under a wooden canopy had seen better days. "It's paid for, has an engine, and will get us anywhere we point the bow. I've had her for going on…well, er, about twenty-five years."

"How old is the engine?"

"It's had repairs."

Rob had severe doubts. The rickety craft looked no more reliable than Delroy's old sedan. "I don't mind chartering a bigger boat."

"If you want something fancy, sure thing. I'll check at the office. Be back in a few." Delroy headed up the pier, leaving Rob behind.

The sun beat down on Rob as he surveyed the older vessels creaking like arthritic joints in the gentle wakes created by boats traveling out to sea. Delroy returned to the dock as Rob ended the call. "Sorry, no boats available. Too many tourists." The boat wobbled as the detective climbed into his vessel and donned a life jacket that fit around his neck like a kiddie collar. "We always wear safety gear on my boat. I ain't taking no chances."

Hmm. Rob studied Delroy's ill-fitting vest.

"How about unhooking the rope mooring us to the dock, and I'll steer?" Delroy tossed Rob a life jacket.

Rob donned the orange vest before unwinding the thick rope from a post. He jumped into the vessel and sat on the seat opposite Delroy's.

The detective started the motor and operated the wheel. When the boat reached the open sea, he gunned the engine. The vessel made noises like a worn-out veteran but picked up a little speed. Delroy finally peered over his sunglasses. "Read me the coordinates, and I'll point the bow in the right direction."

After digging in his pocket, Rob handed him the scrap paper. "Will it take long to reach the first island?"

Delroy glanced at the paper. "Nah."

"Not sure I can handle these waves." The rocking boat and engine fumes made him nauseous. But he'd endure anything for Sloan and Vivi.

Chapter Eighteen

As the sun's rays filtered through the curtains over a window, Jameson closed his book and snuffed the candle. The large steroid doses had done their job. The lady hadn't displayed abnormal symptoms for several days. She'd talked about someone named Rob in her sleep though. *Was it possible to keep her memories from returning?*

Jameson rose from the comfortable sofa and paused for a last glimpse of her while she slept. He understood her irritability. Steroids often caused bad moods. He'd been on them in the hospital while recuperating.

One day, he hoped to take her for late-night walks on the beach. He had so much to share with her, but first, she'd have to feel comfortable in his presence. Yet she'd likely run away if given the opportunity. Since her memories were returning, time was running short to win her favor.

Movement stirred under her bedcovers. As she sat up in bed, he lurched behind the partition and and observed her through a hidden mesh embedded in the decorative screen. "Good morning, Miss."

Startled, the lady clutched the bedcovers. "How long have you been here?"

"Through the night, but just to made sure you're okay. You seem so, but Dr. Boyd wants your activity limited for another week—there's a chance of rebound swelling in your brain."

The lady released the covers and scanned the room. "Where is this nefarious doctor who refuses to appear?"

Jameson resisted the urge to laugh at her absurd remark. "No, no, no. Dr. Boyd is a respectable gentleman. We'll visit him soon."

"At least ease my anxiety. Tell me why you hide." Her piercing eyes bored a hole in the screen.

Escalating abdominal pain forced Jameson to slide on a stool behind the partition. How much of his story could the lady handle? If she exhibited fear, he'd have to stop. "Let me think where to begin." His voice quivered as he spoke.

"Five years ago my fiancé, Veronica, flew to Paradise Island after I returned from combat duty in the Middle East. But my efforts to prepare her failed." An uncomfortable pause ensued, and he drew a jagged breath. Talking about Veronica always triggered PTSD—since that horrible day. He tamped down his rising fears.

"At the time, my wounds were fresh—raw—if you will. I had been discharged home from a hospital in Germany where the Marines flew me for surgery after a debilitating injury. Bandages secured by gauze covered my face and head. I expected Veronica to welcome me. Comfort me. Or, at least, show a little compassion or empathy. But the fear in her eyes shattered my spiraling self-image. I explained the injury, but shock clouded her ability to comprehend."

Jameson's lungs filled with fiery pain as he struggled for another deep breath. "At night, she stole into my room and lifted the bandages. I turned my head to face her, thinking it was Nicholas, but she began screaming.

'No, Veronica, no!' I shouted. But it was too late." He pressed his fist over his mouth, holding back the sobs heaving his chest.

"Veronica fled from my room without allowing me to explain. When Nicholas heard her screams, he rushed to my room and tore after her, but he found her collapsed on the beach."

Jameson's breaths came too deep, too rapid—hyperventilation had set in. Air hunger took over. Another panic attack. Passing out would follow if he didn't get it under control. But the lady might rush behind the screen to help and discover his secret.

"Bear with me, Miss. I'll continue in a minute." He held his breath as long as possible to equalize his carbon dioxide level. The technique had stabilized his breathing in the hospital.

When his ability to inhale returned to normal, he continued. "Thank you for your patience."

"Take your time," the lady said. "There's no rush."

"I'd like to finish. When Nicholas found Veronica, he begged her to return to the mansion, but she sobbed and refused to discuss the situation. She left Paradise Island and never returned. Her behavior sent icy terror through my veins. I vowed never to show myself to another human being."

"I'm so sorry. Did your wounds heal?"

"Yes and no." Jameson struggled to catch his breath again. "Some things will never heal." The gnawing abdominal pain doubled him over and his galloping heartbeat and burning lungs threatened imminent physical demise if he continued speaking.

"Please explain. I'll understand."

A rap struck the door.

"I've given you much to process, Miss. Please enjoy your meal." He gripped his midsection as he slipped

through the door and past Nicholas without looking back.

Chapter Nineteen

Nonstop questions hounded Sloan after hearing Jameson's frightening tale. When would she meet the man who called her Miss? The least he could do was allow her to draw an honest conclusion about his appearance and decide whether to stay or ask for a trip home, wherever that may be. Considering Jameson's pleasing voice and attractive build, why would he need to hide? His positive characteristics seemed to outweigh any negatives.

At that moment, another voice, deeper, sexier, broke through her veiled memories as it had the day before. A dark-haired man teased her, and they laughed together as though they shared a relationship. If only she could recall his name and the details, but the memory remained fuzzy.

She ran her hand over the romance books stacked on her bedside table. The stories filled her with a longing for companionship. The last three days had seemed like forty since the brothers locked her in her room. *Hadn't she suffered enough? How much longer until she lost her mind?*

As the afternoon sunlight poured through the windows, she stared at the tropical trees and flower bushes outside. Closing her eyes, she imagined walking on the sandy beach in the distance, the sea's gentle waves warming her ankles, and its salty perfume stirring her emotions. Since her captors ignored her pleas, she'd have to devise an escape.

Leaning against the bed, she removed the snug elastic wrap from her foot. The swelling had subsided, and a mustard tint replaced the purple bruising. On standing, she nearly applied equal weight to both feet. With additional tight wraps, she might tolerate walking.

The door's lock clicked.

Nicholas strolled into the room, his silky hair brushing his shoulders. Sloan wondered if he resembled Jameson. Did his brother possess his same strong jawline and slender yet manly nose?

Nicholas carried a tray topped with a teapot and cup alongside a plate of sliced honeydew and cantaloupe. A pill lay on the napkin. "Would you care for tea, Miss?"

"I'd rather enjoy the sunlight outdoors."

"I understand. But Dr. Boyd insists you must heal first."

"I've heard those words too many times. I'm going mad inside these walls."

"I'll inform the doctor, though I'm not sure he'll change his mind." Nicholas strode to the door and glanced both ways down the hall before leaving.

Had Jameson been listening?

A hazy flashback came to mind. A man in a white medical jacket. But the vague memory wasn't much help for Sloan's current situation.

She hobbled to the sofa and poured tea from the lavender teapot into its matching porcelain cup. The steaming peachy scent calmed her nerves, and the honey-infused sip soothed her throat. Another gulp and she swallowed the pill.

As she sat back and enjoyed the brew, her eyes wandered over the surroundings. Someone had placed new photographs on the mantel while she slept. The thought unnerved her, but she limped to the fireplace. A second photo of a handsome man in military fatigues drew her attention because a woman rested against his chest. His arms encircled hers as he nuzzled her flowing chestnut hair. The woman smiled, obviously filled with happiness. Were they Jameson and Veronica? Why would such a contented woman abandon her love over war injuries? It made no sense.

Sloan replaced the photo and studied the other three pictures. Small boys in team shirts and shorts held soccer balls while standing side by side in two pictures. She assumed they were young Nicholas and Jameson. In the last photo, the tow-headed teens curled weights and showed off their muscled biceps. They resembled one another in many respects.

Jameson's refusal to show himself saddened Sloan. He'd monitored her condition for several nights, giving up sleep and comfort without thanks. She yearned to learn more about his kind heart and soothing voice.

The key clicked in the lock.

Nicholas reentered the room carrying cloth items under his arm. He walked to the coffee table and scooped the tray.

Sloan grasped the photo of the couple and turned from the mantel. "Would you please tell me about this picture?"

Nicholas's demeanor changed from pleasant to guarded. "I snapped it before...before..." His eyes clouded with tears.

"You don't have to discuss it if it's too painful." Sloan examined the items in his hand. "Are those for me?"

He showed her the clothing. "Yes. They belonged to...her. She was about your size. Try them on if you would. I'll wait to make sure they fit before I leave. If they're too big, I can provide more." Nicholas handed her the shirt and blouse.

Had Veronica left the island without her belongings? Odd. Maybe it was best if Sloan didn't meet Jameson face to face. She hobbled to the en suite and donned the clothing, a bit nervous about wearing Veronica's possessions. Standing before the mirror, she admired the V-neck blouse and thigh-length skirt. "They fit well. Thank you," she called to him.

"I have a surprise for you tonight, Miss," Nicholas's said from the bedroom.

Sloan's heart raced as she exited the en suite and found him gone. *What did he have in mind?*

Chapter Twenty

The sun's gentle rays crept through the blinds, gently coaxing Rob from his sleep without success. *A tropical breeze caressed his skin as he lounged on a Caribbean beach.*

He opened his eyes. *It had been a dream. Sloan.* The harsh reality of her disappearance punched him in the gut. The situation was as real as the knotted covers on his bed. Dawdling wouldn't help him find her. He had to meet Delroy downstairs for another day at sea.

Feeling the dizzying aftereffects of yesterday's churning waves, he forced himself up from the plush bed and staggered to the en suite. Within seconds the shower's cold spray jolted him awake. He washed, then donned the bathroom's soft white robe, walked to the cottage's door, and opened it. A fresh set of clothing in a bag lay on the doorstep. Thankful for the hotel's commitment to their guests, he donned the ebony tee and khaki shorts. While not his typical style, he appreciated an improvement from the soiled clothing he'd worn for the last two days. After changing, he glimpsed his image in a wall mirror and winced at the whiskers staring back at him. The rugged appearance was a stark contrast to his usual clean-shaven face. Too

tired to care, he trudged to the lobby and on to the Crested Quail.

A talkative hostess with pink-tipped hair greeted him at the pub's reception counter. Rob managed a nod at her bubbly welcome. "I'm here for breakfast with someone," he said.

"Please follow me." The lady placed a menu on a table and disappeared.

Rob pulled out a chair and settled on the seat, but his rhythmic shoe tapping on the marble floor echoed throughout the quiet room. Thoughts of returning to sea—in Delroy's boat—made him want to fly home or do anything except suffer more waves and engine fumes, but he couldn't give up on Sloan.

As he waited for the detective, a server with a nose ring approached his side, carrying a steaming brew in a glass carafe. "Would you care for some coffee?"

"I could use a pot full. Maybe two."

She chuckled as she raised an upside-down cup from the table and poured. He closed his eyes and inhaled the brew's robust aroma. When she finished, he enjoyed a hearty sip of the strong caffeine. "Ahh. Delicious."

"We have an excellent breakfast buffet," the waitress said. She motioned to a counter with silver serving dishes. "Unless you'd like something on the menu."

Rob wasn't hungry. And Delroy was nowhere in sight. After ordering food and more coffee for the road, he called the detective. "Morning, Delroy. Ready for sea duty?"

The detective mumbled, "I-uh-um-er-will-er-do-so, boss," obviously still asleep.

Rob's shoulders slumped as he pocketed his cell phone. Seconds ticked by as he waited, and every wasted minute placed Sloan's life in danger.

Chapter Twenty-One

An hour later Delroy's vintage sedan pulled up to the lobby doors and shimmied after it stopped. Rob marched to the car carrying a sizable to-go bag wafting fresh coffee and yeasty cinnamon roll scents. He opened the passenger door before the detective climbed from the vehicle. "Glad you made it, Detective."

"Overslept a little. No problem, boss."

Rob ground his teeth at Delroy's sluggish speech. He would have slept in, too, *if lives weren't at stake.* But they were.

The detective rubbed the sleep from his eyes and sighed, letting the air out of his lungs in measured breaths.

Heat traveled up Rob's neck. Plenty of detectives worked on the island. He'd left the list in his cottage. He thudded into the passenger seat and slammed the door so hard the car rattled. "I'm glad it's not a problem for you, Detective, but it is for me." Rob rarely lost his temper, but he'd been through enough on the island to reach a boiling point.

Clad in the same ragged suit he'd worn since Rob met him, Delroy removed the cigar from his pocket and rolled it under his nose.

Rob felt hot lava ready to burst from his temporal arteries. The detective had some nerve ignoring him. "If you're not up to sleuthing, I'll pay for services rendered and find someone else."

"Sorry, boss. Investigating isn't the problem. As I've said, finding two ladies in the Caribbean is like searching for gems in the vast sea."

"I won't give up. And I'll not leave here until I locate them or learn what happened."

Delroy tucked the cigar inside his jacket. Without warning, he slammed the gas pedal to the floor, sending Rob flying back against the seat as the old car tore over the resort road. Rob couldn't believe the old clunker or Delroy, for that matter, had it in them.

Both men sat in silence as the car swerved onto the marina's dirt road and screeched to a stop. Shaken from the testosterone-fueled ride, Rob staggered from the vehicle. "How about if we tuck our egos into our waistbands and charter a bigger boat for today?"

"They're all booked, boss. I called earlier." Delroy plodded to the dock, Rob at his side.

When they reached the boat, Rob tossed him the sack. "I bought enough lunch and snacks for the entire day." He untethered the boat and hopped into the vessel.

Delroy inhaled deeply as he peered inside the bag. "Umm, smells good." He placed the food in the stern's storage area before keying the ignition and riding the wakes away from the marina.

Rob fished the worn scrap of paper from his pocket and read the coordinates for their first stop. In short order, they arrived at a seashore where an aging gentleman greeted them from a beach chair. He raised a tall glass filled with a pink beverage. "Welcome, friends!"

"Hello, sir." Rob waded to the sand. "I'm Rob Ambrose."

"Nice to meet you. I'm Elliot Fletcher, old chap."
The man gestured theatrically as he spoke. His vocal
delivery reminded Rob of James Earl Jones's deep,
resonant tone. "I was once a British Shakespearean actor
in my prime. You might recognize me from King Lear
and Richard III on the big screen, but they're just a
smattering of my movies."

"It's nice to meet you, sir. If you don't mind, I'll get to
the point about our mission. We're searching for two
young ladies who might have washed ashore on your
island."

"No one has washed ashore here. My staff and I are
the only inhabitants. Scour the island in my jeep if you'd
like and join me for afternoon tea."

Rob appreciated his offer, but searching the island of
a distinguished aging actor seemed unproductive.
However, Delroy waded to the beach and insisted they
ride over the dunes and search for hidden evidence the
ladies had been there. "Don't trust no one, boss."

"Given Fletcher's advanced age, I believe him."

"You trust those you don't know? Living around here
might change your mind. Remember Trinidad, the scam
artist?" Delroy sat shotgun while Rob drove the jeep over
the uneven sandy terrain, but the lengthy drive around
the island failed to produce information about Sloan and
Vivi.

Skipping tea, Rob and Delroy returned to Delroy's
boat and explored several uncharted islands that Fletcher
suggested they visit. At Rob's prompting, the detective
stopped at each one, but their searches proved futile.

As the sun neared the horizon, water began bubbling
through a floorboard in the hull. "We've got water in the
boat, Detective. I thought you said this thing is
seaworthy."

"It needs a good caulking, but it's solid. Should get us
home even if there is a little leak."

Little leak? Rob scooped a pail full and showed Delroy the contents. "If the water gets too high, will it flood the engine?"

"Yes, boss. If the engine floods, my boat is going down."

"Does that mean we're goners?"

"Maybe." Keeping one hand on the helm, Delroy removed the cigar from his pocket and studied the stogie before turning his attention to the inch-deep water covering the hull. He placed the stogie between his teeth and pulled a match from his pocket.

"Stop! Don't do it, Detective."

"You'd better bail faster then, boss."

Chapter Twenty-Two

Nicholas returned a few hours later with an ebony stick tucked under his arm. "I thought this might come in handy."

It definitely would. Sloan's posture stiffened as she quieted her delight. He'd kept the cane from her, but now, she had the key element for a plan she'd been devising.

Nicholas interrupted her thoughts. "Would you care to join me in the dining room?"

Sloan could barely contain her excitement. If she were alone, she'd squeal with happiness. "What a wonderful surprise. I'd enjoy leaving this room."

Nicholas offered her his arm for support, and she limped from the room using the poker for support. She admired the coastal art on the walls and the light wood flooring as they walked down the hallway. Nicholas led her to a beach-inspired dining room with an oval white pedestal table and six sea-blue chairs. Her gaze rested on a wall picture—seagulls perched on wooden beach chairs. Frothy waves lapped the sand. "This is beautiful."

"Indeed, it is." Nicholas helped her settle into a chair before taking a seat beside her. "Our cook will bring dinner soon."

"Will Jameson join us?"

"I'm sorry. Panic attacks prevent it. Except for his doctor, August Boyd, the staff and I rarely saw him for years, but Jameson moves around our home freely now, interacting with the staff. It'll take time for him to feel comfortable with you."

"Please tell me what happened." Sloan's voice strained as she pleaded for information. The elusive Jameson's secrecy drove her to distraction.

"As I've mentioned, it's not my story to share." Nicholas's hands quivered as he rested his elbows on the table.

"At least explain why he needs a doctor."

"I suppose my brother wouldn't mind a disclosure about his abdominal pain. He suffers from radiation poisoning."

"What happened? Is there radiation on the island?"

"We're safe. Jameson will elaborate before long."

"Nicholas, how do you stay sane around here without global communication? Aren't you bored?"

"Not too often. We have activities—courts for volleyball and basketball, a bowling alley, and a home movie theater. We also ride bikes and horses for transportation and have a horse-drawn carriage and wagon, but surfing is our favorite pastime."

"If there's no electricity, how do you watch movies?"

"With a battery-powered DVD player. We have an entire bookcase stocked with movies."

The cook interrupted them carrying dinner plates laden with butter-braised lobster tails, fragrant yeasty biscuits, and steamed asparagus. Sloan's stomach grumbled as she examined her plate.

Nicholas poured water from a pitcher into their glasses and waited for her to take a bite. Elbows resting on the table, he twisted his glass stem, his eyes glowing in the candlelight.

Sloan dipped a lobster chunk in butter and savored it in her mouth. The cook paused behind Nicholas, angling her head at Sloan. "I've been eager to learn how you're doing, Miss. When you arrived at the mansion, Ivy Boyd and I bathed and dressed you."

"Your kindness means a lot to me. I can't thank you enough, but how did I get here?"

"The brothers brought you in the horse-drawn wagon. Your hair was a mess—mucked with sand and dried blood. We removed the majority, but rinsing the grit from your mouth was quite a chore."

"I'm much better, thank you."

Nicholas motioned to the cheerful lady. "This is Cook, also known as Esther Sims."

Esther nodded. "Please enjoy your dinner. I left dessert in the kitchen. If you're satisfied, I'll be off." She smoothed the apron covering her simple sundress before returning to where she'd come.

Sloan and Nicholas helped themselves to the mouthwatering meal. "Delicious. Did you catch the lobster?" Sloan asked.

"We all snare the lobster, catch fish, and hunt one or two days a week. My brother brought the quail to the island when we first arrived. They would've overpopulated the land by now except for—well, I'll tell you about Old Fella another day." Nicolas cleared his throat, his eyes downcast. After a few seconds, his sour mood lifted. "We give Esther the credit for our meals. She's an excellent cook."

"I heard that," Esther hollered from somewhere in the house.

Nicholas's lips curved into a playful smile. "Did I ever tell you that we have vast gardens and orchards?"

"I don't believe so, but I'd enjoy seeing them."

"We'll make it happen soon."

Sloan delighted in every morsel on her plate. Although she enjoyed the time away from her room, it did nothing to quell her anxious energy. She knew the risk in her plan but was determined to see it through.

She slid the sharp place-setting knife under her napkin as she finished her meal. Without making a to-do, she placed the utensil inside her skirt band and covered it with her blouse. It was the second most important item for her plan.

The dinner conversation changed to books, a topic Sloan enjoyed but couldn't remember why. Nicolas reported having read each novel she'd found in her room. "Pride and Prejudice by Jane Austen is my favorite," he said.

Excitement filled Sloan. "I finished it last night."

They discussed feisty Elizabeth Bennett's behavior and the brooding Fitzwilliam Darcy as they ate Esther's delicious dessert—fresh coconut milk, banana, and date pudding topped with coconut whipped cream.

"At first, I disliked Mr. Darcy." Sloan licked her spoon. "But my opinion changed when I learned how he helped people behind the scenes."

"I respected how he secretly paid off Mr. Wickham's debts and arranged for him to marry Lydia to save face for the Bennet family. Mr. Darcy's generosity stood out to me." Nicholas deposited a spoonful of pudding in his mouth and raised an eyebrow for Sloan to continue the conversation.

She pondered the story for a few seconds. "I can't remember many details."

"As you mentioned, Mr. Darcy helped people. Jameson is like him. He's insecure and socially inept, but he has a big heart and cares about people."

Nicholas's words compounded the intrigue surrounding his brother, but Jameson's refusal to show himself didn't endear him to her.

During the lengthy dinner, Nicholas treated Sloan as a guest instead of a prisoner. She appreciated his company, but after finishing the dessert, she placed her napkin on the table.

"Are you tired? I'll help you to your room." He rose from his seat and waited for her to stand. "Once your foot and head are healed, we'll escort you around the island."

Was he implying Jameson too? Sloan noticed the lavender elastic band around Nicholas's low-lying ponytail. *Where had she seen it before?*

Chapter Twenty-Three

Sloan reclined on the sofa and considered her plan until a faint "Ahem" behind the screen interrupted her thoughts. "Jameson, are you present?" she called.

"Did you enjoy dinner?"

"It was wonderful."

"I hoped it would brighten your day."

So, had he planned the dinner and not Nicholas? Was he also the one who had gifted her the books? She'd found them on the coffee table one morning.

"Did you notice the additional photos on the mantel?" he asked.

"I did. Are you the man hugging the dark-haired lady?" Sloan balanced with the poker and hobbled to the mantel.

"Yes, he's me before—"

"Will you please share what happened?"

"If you don't mind a lengthy narrative. Make yourself comfortable."

Sloan returned to the sofa and moved a pillow under her head.

"My story dates back to before I enlisted in the Marines. Our family had a pharmaceutical business, and I worked there. Following our parents' demise, Nicholas and I inherited the company and its assets. I purchased this island as a place for us to heal from our grief. We swam, surfed, rode horses, and enjoyed our lives without city stressors and the pharmaceutical company challenges."

"Can I interrupt a second?" Sloan plumped the sofa pillow. "May I ask how your parents died?"

"In a fire that ravaged our home in the States."

"I'm so sorry for your loss."

"I appreciate your kind words. Our parents' deaths were difficult for Nicholas and me. As an escape from our mourning, we joined the Marines to protect innocent lives from nations posing threats to America."

"What a remarkable way to channel your grief. Thank you for your service, but how did you sustain your injury?"

"My men and I received orders to destroy the enemy's ammunition plant. Our intelligence agency learned they awaited plutonium to build weapons for mass destruction. We were to keep the metal from arriving at the premises." Jameson paused for a few seconds.

"One day, my men observed an armed truck hauling a suspicious bin toward the plant. We intercepted it."

Sloan's imagination ran wild, hinging on every word. "What happened?"

"One of my buddies opened the locked bin, and it confirmed our fears—plutonium. I was standing behind the other four. We suffered headaches, nausea, vomiting, and a burning sensation on our skin. My symptoms weren't as pronounced as theirs, but our military doctor handed us a grim diagnosis—radiation poisoning. Within two years, my buddy closest to the metal lost his life to lung cancer. The doctor claimed the rest of us would likely develop cancer in our lifetimes. The situation worried me, but I turned it around for good. If I was going to die young, anyway, I wanted to make it count."

Captivated by Jameson's story, Sloan clenched her hands. "Nicholas told me you were exposed to radiation, but I didn't know the details until now. I'm so sorry. How did you handle it?"

"I joined a Special Operations Force—the Marine Raiders. They're soldiers trained for hazardous duty. Enemy troops had captured several Raiders, and the Marines sent my unit on a rescue mission. Perimeter guards discovered us as we cut through their fence. The tower guard gunned down several of my men before I eliminated him. I'm an expert marksman, able to take out a target at six hundred yards. Once my surviving men and I entered the block house, we fought room to room to free the captured Raiders. Fortunately, the guards were too afraid for their lives to care about the prisoners. They vacated through a window when we came for them in the kitchen, and we saved our Marine buddies. But on a hunch, I performed a final sweep of the building and surprised a guard who had evaded capture. An explosion ripped my face. When I came to, bandages covered my entire head, and I was in a military hospital overseas."

"What happened?"

"The enemy guard shot me in the face."

"Jameson, I'm so sorry. It must have been terrible. Your bravery saved the prisoners, but who rescued you?"

"My first lieutenant returned for me. He carried me from the compound on his back, and a helicopter airlifted us to the hospital. Both Art and I received Purple Hearts. But I didn't need a medal. I would have done it again because my Marine brothers meant the world to me."

"You were very brave."

"I've hidden myself from the world for five long years."

"It's no longer necessary."

"You don't understand. PTSD has tormented me night and day. Veronica had no compassion for my physical or mental status. The nighttime terrors frightened her. If you don't mind, I'll stop for now. The story exhausts me. Perhaps I'll share more tomorrow. Get a good night's sleep, Miss." As he exited through the door, his perfect physique, valiant behavior, and the monstrous looks he professed created conflicting images in Sloan's mind.

But his voice fascinated her. And his picture on the mantle made her swoon. *Why had Veronica run from the house, terrified?* Jameson couldn't be that hideous. Unless he was a liar, charming her before exposing his true intentions.

Chapter Twenty-Four

T he plan, Sloan. Accomplish the plan. She had to stop ruminating over Jameson's unfortunate accident. There was no time to waste. She lingered at the window, assessing the dark clouds and gusty winds. The medicine Nicholas had given her earlier eased the pains in her head and foot. Now, even the weather wouldn't deter her decision.

She had enjoyed the dinner, but tonight, she'd learn her identity even if Jameson freaked out when he learned what she was up to. It didn't matter. The mission would save her sanity.

Sticking to the evening routine, she lit the hurricane lamps in the bedroom. Once the soft glows provided adequate lighting, she collected the poker and the knife hidden in her waistband. Taking care not to make noise, she drew back a gauze curtain and checked for household members on the beach. Only the sea's roar broke the silence.

Quickly, she cut three edges of the screen's frame with the knife, moved the mesh aside, and climbed on the ledge. As she peered at the ground, it appeared steeper than she'd imagined. Doubts hindered her thinking. If she landed on her sore foot, the injury might worsen, and she might have trouble reentering the house. But she

refused to consider the alternative—abort the plan. It wasn't an option.

She held her breath, threw the poker from the window, and pushed off the ledge. Her good leg hit the ground with a thud. Instinctively, she crumpled on her side to protect the opposite limb. Joy filled her heart. She was free. But there was no time to revel in her escape or her surroundings. She had to move quickly before Nicholas made his final rounds for the night.

After retrieving the poker, she straightened and half-walked, half-ran up the beach. By the time she distanced herself from the mansion, the winds had picked up, but she didn't care. She fought through the pain and traveled another fifty feet, then a hundred feet, until she cried out in pain and could go no further. A gusty wind sprayed saltwater over her face as she crumpled to the sand.

On the horizon above the sea, a tiny light flickered. A boat? A motor's roar confirmed her thoughts. She rose from the sand and waved overhead. "Help! Please, rescue me!" Darkness cloaked her body and wind muted her calls. If she'd brought a lantern, she could have signaled the vessel. She shouted again, "Help! Rescue me!" But the boat continued on course.

Chapter Twenty-Five

Rob's shoulders ached, and spasms twisted his arm muscles as he heaved another water-filled bucket overboard. "Detective, did you send out an SOS?"

"Tried to, boss, but my radio isn't working."

Rob scooped another pail and hurled the water overboard before shouting over the wind and waves, "Doesn't anything in the Caribbean work?"

"Scarlett Bay citizens aren't wealthy, boss."

Poverty explained the shacks, threadbare clothing, and vehicles from the '80s. "Can you take over bailing?" Flaming pain tortured Rob's entire body.

"I'm on it, boss." Delroy stepped down from the helm into water covering his shoes. "This doesn't look good." He searched the sky. "There's a storm brewing too. We'd better get back pronto."

Rob tossed him the bucket. The detective began bailing as fast as he gulped air.

Overhead, the swirling clouds gained speed, forcing Rob to reassess their situation. If the waves grew any higher, they'd swamp the deck. He'd read about powerful and dangerous currents surrounding islands. What if they sucked Delroy's boat farther out to sea or washed the detective and Rob overboard? Rob checked

his life jacket and found the top and bottom straps secure. The last thing he wanted was to become fish food.

He sloshed through the water, raising his knees to his chest for each step toward the helm. On a hunch, he checked the storage unit in the stern. It contained ropes and tools. "Are there any more buckets?"

The detective hurled water overboard. "One of us has to steer so we don't go off course." He returned to bailing without significantly reducing the surging water. But despite wheezing, he gave the task his all.

Swells rose from the sea's surface and resembled miniature white-capped mountains. Their sharp peaks were jagged and threatening. Rob's muscles screamed as each rising wave folded and sucked the boat lower and lower. "What can we do, Delroy? I'll never find Sloan if we sink."

Delroy resembled a pressure cooker ready to explode, and his jagged breathing didn't help. Despite his fatigue, Rob motioned for the bucket. "Here, you steer. I'll try bailing again."

Delroy crawled to Rob as a whitecap broke over the bow, drenching them with water. "The sea spells trouble tonight, boss."

"What about Fletcher's island?" Rob shouted over the waves. "We could stay at his place tonight. He might have a spare boat too."

"Too late. Same distance there as it is to Scarlett Bay. We might as well move forward."

"Look, do you see those?" Rob stretched his arm and finger toward the flickering lights on his left.

Delroy inhaled a deep breath. "Could be Paradise Island. Best not to anchor there. It's one of those dangerous islands." He scanned the boat for the umpteenth time. "Wish I had a patch for this crack. At least it's not getting any bigger." He stepped to the helm and steadied the bow toward Scarlett Bay.

An unexpected wave lifted the boat higher and higher before crashing it into the sea. The extreme force cracked more boards in the hull. Foamy water gushed into the boat and Rob's nightmare worsened.

"Ship's going down!" Delroy shouted. He grabbed two life preservers and half-swam, half-ran through the calf-high water to the stern where he opened a compartment and snatched a survival kit. "You'll need this." He tossed Rob a life preserver and placed the other one under his arm.

Rob caught the ring. "Are there sharks in this area?"

"Can't talk. Gotta abandon ship."

The water in the hull slapped at Rob's knees.

Gripping the kit and preserver, Delroy climbed over the side first.

Rob's calf struck a sharp metal toolbox lid as he forced his legs through the water to reach the spot where the detective had gone overboard. Blood ran down his leg. He stared into the choppy sea and wondered if this was the end of his life. He pushed off the side and landed in the water as a wave broke over his head. He bobbed back up and searched frantically for the detective. "Delroy?" He spat water. "Delroy, where are you?"

Chapter Twenty-Six

Sloan fell to the sand, exhausted from her efforts to alert the boat. After resting, she gazed up the shoreline. A flickering light came into view. She rose and brushed the sandy grains from her skin and clothing.

Tightening her grip on the poker and gritting her teeth, she limped over the sand, determined to satisfy her goal. The light ahead shined brighter, showing her the way. She squinted and made out a silhouette. Was it a home? Would she find the other survivor before the brothers found her? Her heart pounded like a kettledrum as fiery pain shot up her leg, but she quickened her pace, determined to accomplish her mission. Soon the structure became apparent—a cottage.

Could it be Dr. Boyd's home? Newfound hope encouraged her to keep up the pace, and the escalating winds pushed her along. She moved faster up the beach, hop-running, digging the crutch into the sand and toe-touching her injured limb to the ground for balance. Huffing and puffing, she arrived at the cottage, hoping it belonged to Dr. Boyd.

A man and two women stood in front of a picture window inside the home. Bracing her throbbing foot, Sloan crept behind a cart near the front door. She peered around it to watch the figures inside the home. The dark-haired woman's movements suggested she was a young adult. The second lady, whose squat body and slow motions depicted an older woman, walked between the younger lady and the man. They were engaged in an animated discussion.

She crept from the cart to the picture window, biting back foot pain. Muffled voices reached her ears. "Nicholas...Walkie-Talkie," the deeper voice said. "Other lady...mansion... find her."

"Take...with you...Dr. Boyd," a woman's voice pleaded.

Adrenaline filled Sloan's veins and commanded her to hide or flee. She had accomplished her mission to find Dr. Boyd's home, but he was coming for her. She hobbled away from the window, her fears escalating. But the plan, the whole reason she came to the cottage, stopped her. She had to meet the other survivor and learn her identity.

Her stomach knotted as she turned and limped closer and closer to the porch. Unable to see clearly, she stumbled over a tree branch in her path. The poker flew from her hand. It struck the cement porch, and a metal pinging sound echoed through the night air.

The door opened and a gray-haired man shouted, "Who is out there?" The lantern in his hand swung as he spun around.

Caught like an unsavory intruder, Sloan crawled to the poker and dug it into the ground. She stood and faced the porch. "It's me. The lady Jameson and Nicholas rescued."

The man aimed the lantern at her and inspected her form. "Nicholas alerted me you'd left. I must take you back."

"Can I meet the other survivor who washed ashore? I mean, your guest?" Sloan attempted to move around the man to the door, but he blocked her path.

"Meeting isn't advisable. Undue excitement might worsen your head injury."

Sloan cringed at his words because her "condition" had improved. "If you allow me to talk to your guest, I'll gladly..."

The man barred her from getting past him, but the door opened, and the young dark-haired lady walked onto the porch behind him. "Go back inside," he shouted at her.

His shoulders prevented Sloan from seeing the woman's face. "Stress from not having answers hurts my brain worse than if I were to meet someone." Sloan used her elbows and the poker stick to bypass the man.

The older woman appeared through the door and shuffled the young lady into the house. She closed the door behind them.

Sloan again attempted to bypass the man to reach the door. "Please, I beg you, let me meet the lady. Maybe she'll recognize me."

Chapter Twenty-Seven

A hand appeared above the water. "I'm over here!" Delroy's head and neck, buoyed by his miniscule orange life jacket, rose and dipped in the water.

Fighting against the choppy waves, Rob finally reached the detective's side. "I'll tie our life preservers together," he shouted.

Delroy raised a flashlight for him. "Take this. I'll keep...flare gun." A wave splashed over his head, and he sputtered water after it passed.

Rob accepted the light after tethering himself to Delroy. The rough waves made the endeavor challenging, but he feared for Delroy's survival if they drifted away from each other.

With his head back and eyes closed, the detective mumbled, "Save us, Lord." The wind and waves distorted his words, but he repeated them many times.

Rob swam toward Scarlett Bay's lights, towing Delroy by the ropes, hoping he wouldn't glance over his shoulder and find the detective submerged. Suddenly, a blinking light appeared, followed by a muffled engine roar. Rob aimed the flashlight and shouted, "Help! We're over here."

He retrieved the flare gun from Delroy and fired a blazing light at the sky. "Help us!" Rob shouted again.

A horn sounded from an incoming vessel, and a searchlight swept the sea.

"We're over here!" Rob shouted. "Help!"

Delroy opened his eyes. He gulped water as he opened his mouth. A wave covered his head, but the life preserver kept him afloat.

Rob shone the flashlight on him as the white yacht approached. "Don't give up!" Rob slapped the detective's cheeks. "Wake up, Delroy. Help is here."

A few minutes later, the yacht idled near them. A giant man leaned over the railing and tossed two life rings. "Grab these. I'll pull you in by the ropes."

Rob worried the detective's impaired breathing coupled with his intense struggle in the waves made him susceptible to a heart attack. He caught a ring and placed it over the detective's head and one arm. "Hold tight, detective." He released the slipknot joining them. "Reel him in!" Rob shouted to the yachtsman.

The yachtsman threw a rope-type ladder over the side and began reeling Delroy in. As the detective neared the ladder, the man dove into the sea and dragged him to the boat. The detective gripped the ladder. Using his shoulders, the yachtsman pushed the exhausted detective up the rungs.

Satisfied Delroy was on his way to safety, Rob swam for the second life ring, but a fin surfaced. "Shark! help!" He grabbed the ring and tugged it over his head and arms. "Pull me in!" The fin began circling him. Rob swam double-time toward the ladder.

As Delroy reached the ladder's top rung, the yachtsman heaved him overboard by the waistband, jumped aboard, and returned to the railing. He gripped Rob's rope. "I'm reeling you in, buddy. Swim!"

Using every ounce of strength he could muster, Rob sped through the water until his hands reached the ladder's rungs. The shark's gray body, striped with dark bars, surfaced behind him.

"It's a fourteen-footer, at least. Hurry!" the yachtsman hollered.

An enormous wave splashed Rob on his second step up the ladder. "Don't turn around. Keep climbing!" the yachtsman shouted.

Chapter Twenty-Eight

The man on the porch grasped Sloan's arm and dragged her down the steps. "Nicholas and Jameson are searching the mansion grounds. You need to go back."

"S-l-o-a—" a muffled woman's voice shouted.

Sloan looked in the picture window and dropped the poker. The matronly woman pulled the young lady through the living room.

"But...but..." Sloan wasn't ready to leave. She hadn't accomplished her mission.

"No 'buts.' I'm Dr. Boyd. I'll escort you to the mansion in my horse and cart. We need to hurry because a storm is brewing."

Under the lantern's light, Sloan noted the lines on the man's face. His thin hair rested below his neck. She grimaced with each step, and he slipped his shoulder under her arm. "Let me assist you," he said.

They reached the wagon, and he lowered a rear panel before lifting her to the ledge. "Can you push yourself inside? I'll secure it once you're settled."

Sloan searched the ground. "Please hand me the fire poker. I need it for support."

He did as she asked, and his demeanor softened. "I've been concerned for you. I don't mean to be harsh, but the Briggs are worried for your safety." He handed her the poker and latched the wagon.

Sloan wiped tears flooding her eyes. Why would everyone prevent her from learning information? "My memories are returning. The other lady might help me fill in the gaps. Does she know why we crashed?"

"Calm down, Miss. Some people lose their memories for years, and some never regain theirs. Your memory loss might be from amnesia or from a conversion reaction to having crashed. There will be time for visits with my guest later. For now, let's not place undue stress on your situation. Besides, we must not keep the Briggs waiting. Give me a minute to harness my horse."

Dr. Boyd walked behind the cottage and returned minutes later, leading a chestnut horse. He attached it to the cart and climbed to the perch before clicking his tongue. The horse began a slow trot. Sloan muffled her cries on the trip to the mansion. Her disappointment over the turn of events hurt in the one place no one could see. Why couldn't she recall the young lady who survived with her?

The mansion soon came into view. Candles flickered in every window. The brothers had provided beacons for her. When the cart arrived at the back door, Nicholas hurried to meet them. "Thank you, Dr. Boyd." He lifted Sloan from the wagon and set her on her feet. "We were frantic about you, Miss. Wild animals roam this island. It's not safe for you to walk unattended."

Then why wouldn't they take her to meet the Boyds' guest? Sloan couldn't believe the brothers' lengths to keep her in her room. "What kind of wild animals?"

"Crocodiles, for one. We have a swamp running through the island. Old Fella lives there, and he roams the island. We never know when or where he'll appear. I'll escort you to your room." He tipped his head at Dr. Boyd. "Thanks again, Doc. Much appreciated."

"No problem. I'm glad I found her. I'll be heading back to the house. Good night." He snapped the reins, and his horse trotted away.

"Miss, never try to leave the house again. You don't want to make Jameson angry. He has quite a temper."

Nicholas's words floored her. "What would he do?"

"I'm not sure what'll happen tomorrow after this stunt you pulled tonight." He scooped her into his arms. "I think you've done enough walking for today. Hang onto the poker, and I'll carry you to your room." His terse words startled Sloan. He'd never spoken to her in such a manner.

Exhausted, she rested her head on his chest. One minute, the brothers treated her as a guest, and the next, they ordered her around like prison guards.

Nicholas deposited her at the bedroom door. "I believe you can manage from here," he said. He waited until she hobbled inside the room before closing the door.

The lock clicked.

Sloan dropped on the sofa for a momentary rest. After wiping her eyes and pulling herself together, she limped to the four-poster bed and crumpled on the satin comforter. Somehow, she had to learn her identity. *What if others depended on her—a husband or a child? Did she have a connection with the faceless man in her memories? Why couldn't she remember his name?*

Chapter Twenty-Nine

The shark sprang from the water at Rob, its jaw lined with jagged teeth. Rob stared into its mouth, unable to move and unable to speak because of his chattering teeth. The shark dove again.

"Don't give up. Keep climbing!" the man on the yacht shouted.

His words shook Rob from his stupor, but he struggled with the ladder to plant his foot on the next rung—his shaking extremities made the act impossible. He had no traction to drag himself up the ladder without the rung's support. He clung to the ropes, his feet dangling as he held on for dear life.

"If I die, Delroy, save Sloan," he shouted.

The shark's dorsal fin surfaced again and circled beneath the ladder. Rob's foot failed to gain traction on the rung. He spotted the gash on his leg—the reason the shark wouldn't give up.

"Hold tight!" The yachtsman slipped rungs over his biceps and hauled the ladder up with Rob hanging on for his life.

Below Rob, the shark sprang from the water, mouth open, teeth aimed at Rob's legs. The monster chomped the air inches from his foot.

The broad yachtsman hoisted the ladder, bringing Rob closer to the railing. "I've got this," he shouted. He leaned over the side and grasped Rob's shorts. In one swift motion, he hoisted him into the boat.

Rob crashed on the wooden deck alongside Delroy. Although he could barely move, air, glorious air, fueled his lungs. Having been so close to the shark, he could see down its throat had rendered his legs useless. Unknown time passed before he moved, stood, spoke.

He staggered to his feet, but the vessel pitched, causing him to stumble. Arms and feet spread, he fought for balance as the boat continued to list. He shouted over the wind's deafening roar, "Are you okay, Delroy?"

Struggling to catch his breath, Delroy stood but collapsed into a reclining deck chair. "I'll. Be. Fine."

Rob reached the detective and squatted beside him. He placed his fingers on Delroy's wrist. "Your pulse is too fast and irregular. I've seen you do pursed-lip breathing," he shouted over the winds. "Can you do it now?"

Delroy tightened his lips and released a breath in a slow whistle.

"Good. Keep it up." Rob stood and lurched across the deck as western winds whipped him off balance.

The broad yachtsman blocked Rob's trajectory. "We'd better go inside the cabin. Let's help your friend find his sea legs."

Rob and he assisted Delroy inside, and the detective dropped to a bench. "That was quite a daring rescue," Rob said. "We nearly lost our lives out there." He raked the hair from his brow.

"Indeed. They were close calls." The yachtsman pushed a button on his coffee maker. "I'm glad you two survived. I'm Brian, by the way." He clapped Delroy's shoulder before walking to an intercom on the wall. "Cameron, we need to outrun this storm before it gets us. Let's head to the nearest harbor." Static erupted over the intercom. "Right, Dad, but the weatherman issued a warning on the radio. There's a hurricane heading our way."

"Full speed ahead to Jamaica then." Brian clicked off the intercom after his command.

"A hurricane?" Rob had never experienced one. "What should we do?"

"Either sail beyond it before it picks up speed or find a safe harbor." Brian tossed Rob and Delroy oversized towels.

The detective maintained pursed-lip breathing as he dried himself. He removed his suit jacket and reached into its inner pocket before tossing it on the floor. He held up his inhaler and mushy tobacco remnants from his cigar.

"Might want to use your wheezing medicine, Detective." Rob gestured to the device.

Delroy placed it in his mouth and inhaled. After doing so, he passed the water-logged tobacco under his nose.

Brian slid a trash can by his side.

Delroy studied the brown lump in his hand and released a prolonged sigh. "I guess I won't be needing this anymore. I've carried it ever since my doctor told me to stop smoking or plan my funeral." Delroy threw the soggy mess in the can.

"I'll buy you another one." Rob dried his hair with the towel as Delroy gazed at the cigar remains like a lovelorn teenager.

"Thanks anyway, boss. But I might as well let go of it for good." Rob was sure he witnessed a tear rolling down the distraught detective's cheek.

"Let's tend to your wound, Rob." Brian removed bandages from a cupboard and washed and covered the gash. Then he tossed both men plush bath robes from a closet before walking to a coffee pot a few feet away in

the galley. "How did you two get into this situation?" He pushed a button, and the pot began to fill.

Rob explained that Sloan and Vivi were missing. "I'm determined to find them, but we've had a few setbacks. I'm grateful you rescued the detective and me though."

"It's a good thing you shot the flare, otherwise I wouldn't have seen you." Brian filled two coffee mugs and passed them to Rob and Delroy.

Rob tied the robe's belt around his waist before accepting the mug. "When we reach our destination, I'll repay you for these, sir. Would you, by any chance, consider stopping by Scarlett Bay tonight?" He sipped the brew, the steam warming his face.

"Scarlett Bay is a great idea. It's a safe harbor, and this storm isn't letting up." Brian relayed the message to Cameron before opening the refrigerator and removing four sandwiches. "Anyone care for a snack?"

Chapter Thirty

In the shadows of her candlelit room, Sloan lay on the bed's satin comforter, too upset from the evening's events to sleep. Without warning, movement jolted the dressing screen near the door. Imagining her situation hopeless, Sloan mumbled, "Jameson, are you there?" Her barely audible voice matched the depression coating her insides.

"It's late, Miss, but I was concerned for your safety. I'm also afraid your heart is broken."

Where was the anger Nicholas warned her about? *Should she trust Jameson? Did she have a choice?* "Yes, I'm sad. I learned nothing about my identity or my past."

"I understand. I've decided to meet you around the screen where I can better comfort you from your pain."

Sloan's mood changed from gloom to anticipation. She'd get to see Jameson Briggs. She bolted upright. "I'm ready whenever you are."

Movement jostled the screen again in the candlelit room before all became quiet. "I'm going to share hard things, Miss, the most difficult details I've spoken of thus far. Remember the mission I told you about—the-the gunshot to my face?"

"Yes, it must have been terrifying, Jameson."

"Well, the blast...excuse me." The screen buckled, but Jameson set it straight with lightning speed. "I'm sorry. I have to stop shaking."

Sloan wondered whether she could handle the truth, especially since he'd become anxious.

"Let me try again." Rhythmical tapping struck the floor.

Thumps behind the screen knocked it forward, but again, Jameson pulled the partition upright. She squinted to see his face, but the shadows near the door cloaked him in darkness.

"I apologize, Miss. My legs become jumpy whenever I discuss my injuries."

His docile, baritone voice and humility conflicted with Nicholas's bold statement about him possessing intense anger.

"I'll continue," Jameson said, but silence followed his statement until he finally said, "The blast—it–it destroyed my—"

A thump hit the floor. "Are you okay back there?" Sloan wrung her hands. *How could she help him?*

Chapter Thirty-One

Lightning, high winds, and choppy white-capped swells slowed the trip to Scarlett Bay, but the yacht reached the lit marina by midnight. Rob thanked Brian again for rescuing them and vowed to repay him for his kind deeds.

The yachtsman brushed aside Rob's insistence on repayment. "Consider it a good deed. I was at the right place at the right time and glad to help." Rob appreciated the man's humble character and thanked him.

As he and Delroy walked toward the muddy parking lot, he wrinkled his nose. "What's that terrible smell, Detective?"

"Someone probably tossed a dead grouper overboard. Happens often, especially during storms." Staggering on weak legs, the detective located his rusty clunker.

The sedan looked mighty fine to Rob. More appealing than any car he'd ever seen.

"I guess we'll need another boat tomorrow, boss. But I don't have the funds." Delroy wheezed as he dug in his pocket.

Recognizing the detective's exhaustion, Rob offered his palm for the keys. Delroy fell against the car, removed his keychain, and handed it to Rob, who opened the passenger door.

"No problem about a boat," Rob said. "I'll purchase one tomorrow. Something fast and comfortable." He braced Delroy as the detective stepped into the vehicle.

"Sure thing, boss. If the storm allows." Delroy collapsed in his seat, and Rob closed the door.

Hoping the detective was drained and not dead, Rob slid into the driver's side and started the car. "I'm thinking we should check out Paradise Island tomorrow."

Delroy rolled his head to look at Rob. "Sure, if you don't mind ex-military in your face. Gossipers in the Caribbean say Marines live there. And they don't take kindly to visitors. People report dodging bullets when their boats get near the shore."

"The place doesn't sound too promising. Maybe we'll scratch it." Rob pressed the gas pedal.

"Remember when I mentioned some islands are dangerous?" Delroy rubbed his scalp. "In my opinion, Paradise Island tops the list. I'd rather not validate the gossip."

"Duly noted." Rob appreciated the info, but something bugged him about the place. He brushed away the thought. *How could he and an out-of-shape detective resist ex-Marines?*

Chapter Thirty-Two

The commotion behind the screen suggested Jameson had fallen and righted himself from the floor. Sloan wrung her hands, uncertain how to help him.

"Bear with me, please." His voice sounded hoarse, and it quivered worse than it had up to this point.

Did he need water? Sloan lifted the glass from her bedside table and limped to the screen. "Please accept this. I won't peek." She held it for him at the screen's edge.

"Thank you." A hand accepted it.

"Please continue, Jameson," she said. She returned to the bed and waited for him to regain his strength.

"This is quite distressing, but I...what I'm trying to say is...I–I...no longer possess..." He coughed and then cleared his throat. Silence trailed for what seemed like an eternity. "I no longer have...a...a right eye." Floor tapping followed, growing louder and louder. "But the worst part is...the–the explosion...blew away my nose."

Sloan would've buckled to the floor if she hadn't been on the bed. Shock and dizziness overwhelmed her. She'd anticipated facial wounds and burns. But not this. Jameson's injuries were worse than she'd expected. Because of his gorgeous flowing hair and tapered build, she had imagined him a humble Adonis who thought worse of himself than he ought.

But this? She struggled to control her shaking hands. She ached for him. Sobbed deep in her heart for him. He didn't deserve something so horrible.

"To avoid the unsightly appearances, I wear an eye patch over my eye socket, and a metal prosthesis over the cavity that was once…" Silence again. "When my fiancé, Veronica, saw me five years ago, the jagged laceration running down my right cheek was raw. Bandages covered my missing eye, nose, and other facial wounds. The night she stole into my room, I thought she was Nicholas coming to change my bandages. She removed them, and I turned to face her, but she stood there unmoving, her mouth gaping at me. She screamed. And I screamed." Jameson sobbed and Sloan heard shudders rocking his body.

After a minute or two, he continued. "Veronica shrieked down the hallway, and I shouted after her, 'No, Veronica, no!' for what seemed like an eternity, but she fled from my home. Heartbreak, devastation, and truth stormed my soul." Jameson's voice trailed. "And it was the last time I saw Veronica Charmaine."

Sloan clutched her chest. "I'm so sorry."

"After the experience, how could I imagine myself as anything but a monster? The young man inside me conjured images of myself as a grotesque gargoyle. I banished mirrors from my home. Any hopes of a vibrant life fled from my dreams until I found you on the beach. Your presence made me realize hope still flickered in my heart. My mind had begun to bury my dreams in a deep grave, but your interest in me provided optimism. I hoped you might accept me as I am. I still long for my old self—the virile, attractive, desirable Jameson. But I know he's trapped inside a horrible face. It's the worst kind of torture. Imagining a relationship without experiencing one might be the only joy and fulfillment I'll ever receive."

Listening to Jameson's distress, picturing the trauma and excruciating pain he'd endured, capped by his fiance's rejection, was more than Sloan could bear, yet he suffered the anguish daily. He'd lived through more physical and emotional pain than she could conceive. She steadied her emotions to keep from being swept away by his anguish.

"Jameson, I assure you, I won't flee when I see you. Trust me. I'm stuck on this island, so we might as well meet. Why not be friends?"

Had those words come from her mouth? She had swooned over his muscled physique, thinking he was the same gorgeous Marine hugging Veronica in the picture. But now she'd reduced him to a friend? Maybe she wasn't worthy of knowing the valiant Jameson Briggs.

"Prepare yourself, Miss."

Despising her superficial feelings and anxiety, she held her breath and waited.

A flurry of movement occurred behind the screen. Candle flames flickered as he stepped to the middle of the room. He lowered his chin, his hands trembling. Finally, he raised his head.

Sloan gasped.

Jameson spun around to the fireplace. "I'm sorry to have scared you, Miss."

Sloan's heart nearly leapt from her chest. The long, jagged scar on the right side of his face was prominent. A brown eye patch covered his right eye, and a metal prosthesis molded in the identical size and shape of his brother's nose fit where Jameson's nose belonged. Thin straps secured it around his head.

"I didn't mean to gasp." She had girded her nerves, making them rigid with extra resilience, yet her expectations rather than what she witnessed made her gasp. Even though most of his wounds were covered, she wanted to scream and sob over his injuries. He'd endured so much.

He turned to face her, his hands still trembling, his lips folded. "Do you feel like fleeing?"

The seconds ticked as Sloan absorbed the reality before her. Jameson's mouth parted in an uneasy smile, showcasing perfect, milky white teeth. The enemy had maimed Jameson Briggs, but he had sacrificed his safety to save his men and the world from terrorists. Beauty didn't make the man. Character did. And Jameson Briggs had character oozing from every body cell.

"When you didn't respond, I feared the worst. I was ready to hide forever," he added.

"Please forgive me. I had to get used to..." Sloan fretted over her words. No matter what she said, it might offend him.

"I know my image is repulsive. I lost my dreams of marrying, having children, and running my parents' company. I banned mirrors from the mansion for five years, but Ivy and Esther pleaded with me to rehang them. My story exhausts me. Would you mind if I sit on the sofa?"

"Please do. Your wounds don't appall me. They're tastefully covered." Sloan inched to the sofa from her bed and eased down beside him.

"How is your foot?" he asked.

"It's sore and swollen, but it's healing. I can get around."

Jameson left the room but returned moments later carrying a dry ice packet. He squeezed it until it became icy and placed it inside her elastic bandage. "Let's elevate it." He propped her foot on pillows. "Is it better now?"

"Much."

"I'd love to know more of your history, Miss, but we'll have to wait until your memory returns." He placed his arm behind her over the sofa.

Sloan stiffened. *Why did he place his arm there?* She felt uneasy about his boldness. She hoped he wasn't expecting more than she would allow. Or maybe she was misreading his intention. Was he just resting his arm?

She had to pull herself together and show him the same kindness he always showed her. "Tell me about yourself, Jameson. I'd like to know more about your childhood and your parents."

Jameson poured out his story, leaving Sloan smiling at times yet also sad over his parents' deaths and his stint in the Marines. He talked into the early morning hours. When Sloan's head nodded and eyelids fluttered, he carried her to bed and pulled up the covers. The Jameson she'd seen tonight wasn't a monster in appearance or behavior. He was a hero on the battlefield, a man of distinction.

"Good night, Miss." He headed to the door.

"Good night, Jameson." Would she grow accustomed to his face with time?

He closed the door behind him, but something he'd said a few days ago made her bolt upright. *Why was there no way off the island?*

Chapter Thirty-Three

Every frightening moment in the last twenty-four hours—Delroy's sinking boat, the formidable waves, the relentless shark, and Rob's unimaginable fear—threatened to sabotage his mission. Still, he refused to give in to them or his exhaustion. He'd do whatever was necessary to find Sloan.

She would do the same for him, no doubt about it. After losing his first patient during heart surgery, she had comforted him as a workplace friend, reminding him each patient had a unique history and physical limitations, and no one could save the unsavable.

As always, Rob and his OR team had worked tirelessly to save their patient, who happened to be a multimillionaire, but the elderly gentleman's heart had defied repair.

After the failed surgery, Rob's self-confidence plummeted into deep despair. He received a leave of absence from the medical world, but it didn't help. He partnered with wine instead.

As the clinic nurse, Sloan visited him after work. She removed the bottle from his lips, but he lashed out at her. "I'm washed up. I had a good run, but my career is over. Now leave me alone."

But Sloan wouldn't abandon him. She showed up daily despite his behavior. While he languished in self-pity, the television became a mindless distraction. He grieved on the sofa in days-old pajamas, his facial hair growing shaggier by the day. But kind Nurse Sloan came anyway. She called their coworker, Dr. Ethan. He arrived after hospital visits one day and nudged Rob to move over on the sofa. Sitting beside him in all his misery, Ethan watched a TV show.

When the program ended, he clapped Rob on the arm. "So you think you hold the power of life and death?"

Rob grunted and slumped deeper into the sofa cushion.

Ethan turned sideways and curled his leg under his thigh. "You might be a talented surgeon, Rob, but that's where your superpowers end. There's someone far mightier than you, and He's the one who controls everyone's first and last breath, not you."

Rob refused to budge. Ethan squeezed his shoulder and left him smoldering in doubt. Rob spent the evening contemplating his friend's profound statement. The following day, he stopped wallowing in guilt and collected the empty and full alcohol bottles. He deposited them in the trash, and a few days later, he returned to the clinic. After several weeks of therapy, he performed surgery in the operating room.

The phone alarm blared, snapping Rob from his painful memories. He rolled on his side and hit the alarm button. Flames radiated through his aching muscles, and the gash on his leg throbbed. Regardless of his injury, he had no time to nurse pain. Over the past two years, Sloan's sweet kindness had thawed the ice numbing his heart since Liz died. He couldn't bear losing Sloan too.

How long had he slept? He checked his cell phone. Too long. He had to get back to sea. Groaning, he righted himself in bed and scratched his itchy head from the salt water. Too tired to shower, he plodded to the Crested Quail in yesterday's sea-stained black tee and shorts, unbrushed hair, and scruffy beard.

A thirty-something hostess met him at the restaurant's counter with a raised eyebrow.

"I don't usually look this way." Rob squirmed at her steady focus on his attire.

"I don't judge." The lady flipped a long, dark braid over her shoulder. "Follow me."

He trailed behind her as she led the way past tables brimming with morning diners to a small, empty table in the dark recesses of the pub. He deserved the obscure spot, but he hoped the detective would find him.

"Do you need a moment to read the menu?" The hostess asked.

She scanned his clothing and messy hair again. He half expected her to ask if he was a guest in the hotel. She probably wouldn't believe him if he told her he was staying in one of the expensive cottages.

He shook his head in answer to her question. "How about bringing me some buttered toast and extra-hot coffee?"

"I'll let your server know," the hostess said before walking away. Her braid swayed with each slap of her sandals against the floor.

A sob shook Rob's chest, and he stifled it. This turned out to be anything but a vacation. The hostess had led him past the decorated reception room that he'd rented for the special evening with Sloan. Four more colleagues from the Marysville Clinic were supposed to fly in on Friday for the celebration. Rob had planned to propose to Sloan after spending a fun-filled week with her on the island.

He slumped in his chair, his heart tortured by the events of the last three days. Sloan and Vivi were still missing, and he and the detective almost met their doom last night. He wiped his face before releasing a shaky sigh.

Delroy's booming voice snagged him from his thoughts. He looked around the corner and spotted the detective speaking with the hostess before plodding to the buffet. The detective loaded his plate with scrambled eggs, waffles, bacon, and two cheese Danishes, then headed to Rob's table. "Morning, boss. Thanks for breakfast." He groaned as he straddled an empty chair in the same clothes from the last few days. "How are you holding up?"

"I'm tired and achy but determined to keep searching." Rob sipped his coffee and set it down.

Delroy scooped eggs into his mouth, avoiding eye contact. "I think we might need a few days to rest."

"It would be nice, but I don't have time for that. I have to find Sloan and her sister."

"We have a few clues." Delroy sunk his teeth into a Danish. "The guy who owns the transportation and auto shop seemed mighty suspicious, considering what you've told me."

"Easy Joe was very suspicious. When I asked him about two lady tourists, he replied, 'Don't know nothin' about no Mericans.' Funny thing is—I never mentioned they were Americans."

Delroy polished off the Danish. "You and I had the same experience with Kingfish. Remember when I asked him about American tourists, and he responded with 'missing ladies?' I never asked him about ladies."

A young server with dreadlocks arrived at the table, carrying a coffee pot and mugs. She righted the strap on her lime green sundress and raised the carafe to Rob.

After he nodded, she poured the steaming brew. The fresh coffee and bacon aromas from the buffet drifted through the room, almost stirring Rob to eat, but his gut clamped. "How's the buttered toast coming along?" he asked.

The young gal's eyes widened. "I'll check on it." She filled a cup for Delroy before leaving.

A few minutes later, she returned with extra-browned bread.

"You wouldn't know where I can purchase a boat, would you? The coffee's steam wafted up Rob's nose when he lifted the mug. It smelled like caramel, hazelnut, and a bit of heaven. He sipped the smooth liquid, and it warmed his throat.

"I do." She scribbled on a card from her pocket and passed it to him. "Tell mi padre, José, Liliana sent you. He might throw in a discount."

"Thanks." Rob needed a discount about now. He'd been dishing out money like a sailor on shore leave since he'd arrived on the island.

"De nada." She hurried away to a guest who beckoned her.

Rob set his coffee on the table and studied Delroy as he ate. "Have the search helicopters seen anything?" He steepled his fingers and rested them on his lips.

"Nothing. Sorry, boss."

"Are you ready to head back to sea?"

"I ain't goin' to sugarcoat it, boss. My body can only last so many hours. After that, it's kaput." Delroy doubled his efforts and cleaned his plate. "I was dead meat when I hit the bed last night."

Rob pushed his half-burnt toast aside. "Sorry, detective, but we've got over seven thousand islands to search." He hoped Delroy would take the hint and stand to leave.

"Do you plan on searching all of them?" Delroy gulped down his water.

"If I have to." Rob finished his hearty coffee. "Let's go, Detective." He placed enough money on the table for

the meals and a large tip. "Maybe we'll find Sloan today."

Chapter Thirty-Four

Throughout the night, Sloan lay in bed, listening to the terrifying screams and moans echoing from the mansion walls. She pressed a pillow over her head and shuddered, but vivid images of Jameson's broken body writhing in pain filled her mind. PTSD was a horrible affliction. She grieved for him because of the injuries he'd sustained, yet she was happy to have met him and learned his story.

Dawn arrived as she closed her eyes, hoping to find rest from the disturbing night. But the lock clicked in the door.

Nicholas entered the room bearing the usual tray. "Here's your breakfast, Miss."

"Thank you. Leave it on the coffee table. I'll eat later."

Nicholas left the room as swiftly as he'd arrived.

Was he still angry about her leaving the mansion last night? She wouldn't have gone if they'd taken her to Dr. Boyd's house or brought the other survivor to meet her. The brothers were responsible for her escape.

She limped to the sofa and propped her foot on the coffee table as a memory came to mind. A dark-haired man walked by her side in an airport. He placed a cell phone to his ear. "Sloan," he called to her in a deep voice. She focused on his stylish suit and skinny silver tie. He towered over her with a shrouded face. "Sloan," he repeated.

Bubbling with excitement, she hobbled to the windows and parted a curtain. "My name is Sloan," she shouted.

Pungent air carried by a strong wind knocked her from the sill. The turbulent waves had left sea life belly-up on the sand.

Knocks pounded on the door.

"Had someone heard her shout?" She didn't care. She'd discovered her identity.

Jameson opened the door. "Miss, is something wrong?" His voice conveyed a deep concern. "We heard shouting." He glanced back at Nicholas, who halted by his brother's side.

Esther's short bob bounced as she poked her head in the room. "Is everything okay?"

"Yes, I'm fine." But Sloan's voice escalated, gathering more excitement with each word. "Come in. I'll tell you everything."

Confusion furrowed their brows as Jameson, Nicholas, and Esther entered the room. "Please take a seat." Sloan glanced out the window and noticed the sky's swollen gray clouds threatening to downpour at any moment.

Fidgeting with her hands, she gathered the necessary courage to share her revelation. "I've had more memories. This time, they're more vivid." She wanted to dance around the room, to shout at the top of her lungs, but she fought the urge to make a spectacle of her announcement. "I'm no longer anonymous. My name is Sloan." Despite every effort to remain nonchalant, her trembling voice betrayed the swelling excitement within her.

Jameson collapsed on the sofa. "Calm down, Miss. Take this one step at a time. Recalling a name doesn't make it yours."

"But it is my name. I know it." How could she convince him when she sensed it deep inside? "A man hugged me. I walked away from him, but he shouted, 'Sloan!' It's my name. I wish I could see him clearly. He had dark-brown hair and wore a suit. I remember everything but his face."

"Don't push yourself, Miss. Doc Boyd insists it'll take time for brain swelling to resolve." Jameson shot Esther a strange look. "Do we have more dry ice packs?" He raised an eyebrow. "Her trip to Dr. Boyd's house has exhausted her. Maybe her memories are real, and maybe they aren't." Jameson joined Sloan at the window. He placed his hands on her shoulders. "Neurological swelling can cause auditory and visual hallucinations."

Sloan's lip trembled. "Don't you believe me? I'm not seeing things."

Esther eyed Jameson before hurrying from the room, her print sundress rustling over her legs.

What was going on with the three of them? Why did Sloan's memories bother Jameson? She hadn't planned to share them, but how could she not divulge her name?

"You're getting a bit worked up." Jameson steered her to the four-poster bed. "A rest would do you good."

"But I'm not tired."

"Sleep will heal your agitation." Jameson lifted her in his arms.

Sloan wriggled to remove his hands. "Put me down. I'm not agitated, and I'm not a child. Don't tell me what to do."

Jameson laid her on the bed and placed a pillow under her head.

Nicholas walked to the bedside and stood by Jameson, looking down at her. "I have to agree with my brother.

You're worked up. A rest will relax you. You were up with Jameson until late last night."

Esther returned, holding a tray with dry ice packs and a glass of red juice. "Here you go. This will help you calm down. Have a big sip." She placed the beverage near Sloan's lips, her deep smile lines curving around her mouth.

"No juice." Sloan shook her head. "I don't want it."

"What do you mean?" Ester slid it toward her. "You've always enjoyed this beverage."

Sloan turned her head. "Please, everyone, leave me alone."

Nicholas and Esther left the room, but Jameson stayed at her bedside. "Sloan, we want what's best for you. You must believe me." He offered her his hand, but she pulled hers away. His voice quivered, not with the fear he'd displayed when discussing his injuries, but with an apparent apprehension for her well-being.

"I'm tired of the secrecy." She rolled away from him. Was he fearful she'd leave him like Veronica did? As difficult as it had been not to scream last night when he shared his injuries, she'd assured him she wouldn't run away. And she hadn't.

"Look at me, Sloan." She turned her head at his brusque command, and his eyes pierced hers. "Don't try another escape if you know what's good for you." He spoke in a harsh tone she hadn't heard before. "Drink the juice!"

Despite her fears, she did as he commanded.

After she downed the last drop, he stormed from the room.

Chapter Thirty-Five

Delroy inspected the directions on the card Liliana had given Rob. "I know the North Shore Marina. They sell quality boats."

"I hope it's not the place where you bought yours." Rob cracked a teasing smile.

"Good one, boss. No worries. I inherited my boat from my Uncle Eustace."

A few miles down a leafy, palm-lined road, the detective turned into a massive marina filled with fancy yachts, cabin cruisers, speed boats, and small fishing boats. As the car parked, raindrops seeped from the gray clouds overhead.

Delroy exited the vehicle and held up his hand. "Got us a little rain here, boss." He circled his neckline with a finger, pulling the material away from his skin.

After a few yards to the marina's office, the rain began pelting Rob. It changed to a downpour within minutes and soaked his T-shirt and shorts. He needed this about as much as he needed a plantar wart. But at least the deluge kept him awake.

Delroy threw his jacket over his bald head as a man with a cane limped in their direction from a tinted glass building. An umbrella shielded the man from the cloudburst on his approach. "Are you Rob?" He gave them a once-over.

"I am, sir. We've had a few rough days." Rob glanced down at his sea-worn cargo shorts and tee. He and the detective looked like they'd climbed out of an overflowing dumpster on trash day. Rob had a hard time meeting the man's eyes. He'd never gone a day without showering until he began searching for Sloan.

"No worries. I don't judge," the man said. "A sale is a sale if you have the funds. I'm José. My daughter, Liliana, told me you'd be here. We can head to the boats if you're ready."

"We are," Rob said. He and Delroy followed the man to a row of cruisers. "Hey, look at this one, Detective. It's not too big, and the white paint and dark trim are in good shape."

"Yeah, boss, and I bet it had speed—ten years ago." Delroy frowned and scanned more boats.

José steered them to yachts, and they inspected several inside and out until Rob settled on one with speed and extra comfort. A bigger boat seemed appropriate after Delroy's vessel sank.

José's eyes lit up. "You can stay on the sea for days in this baby. Something tells me it's what you need."

"Does she have any problems?" Rob asked.

"Nada," José replied. "She's a year old, repossessed, and good on fuel."

Tired from inspecting boats and wasting valuable time, Rob rubbed the thick stubble on his jaw for a few seconds before declaring, "Okay, I'll take her."

"Now you're talking my language." José led them to an office decorated with expensive wood furniture. "Make yourselves comfortable." He motioned to chairs bordering his desk, then dropped into a padded swivel chair, wrote a figure on paper, and passed it to Rob.

Rob chewed on the inside of his cheek. "Millions? It's a mighty steep price."

"It's the going rate. Inflation and all." José leaned back in his seat. "Besides, I gave you a discount since Liliana sent you."

It didn't look like a discount. Rob massaged the knotted muscle in his neck while debating a decision. He needed safe transportation to navigate more islands per day, and the comfort would be a plus for their long hours. However, he'd deplete a good deal of his savings account. Wasn't Sloan worth every penny? The answer motivated him to act fast. "I'll call my bank and have them transfer the funds. Can I borrow your phone?"

José slid his landline and banking information across the cluttered desk.

After making the call, Rob signed the paperwork.

"I'll have your boat in the sea within a few hours." José shook Rob's hand and gave him the receipt.

After shopping in several establishments for supplies, Rob and Delroy returned to the marina and found the yacht in the water. Rob climbed aboard, placed the food in the refrigerator, and left the binoculars, ropes, clothes for him and Delroy, and other supplies on the floor. After changing into dry clothes, they ate subs before walking to the navigation room. "Would you mind taking the helm, Detective?" Rob handed him the coordinates on the scrap paper from his pocket.

Hopefully, they'd find Sloan today. Rob counted on it.

Chapter Thirty-Six

Wind gusts beat the windows, waking Sloan from her forced nap. She'd made an enormous mistake telling the brothers her name. From now on, she would keep memories to herself.

Reeling with anger, she rang the small bell by her bedside. If the brothers insisted on playing secretive games, she'd do the same. She'd pretend everything was normal, or as normal as possible with Jameson's mysterious nature. His stern manner when he commanded her not to try another escape "if she knew what was good for her" sent Sloan's arm hairs on end.

The door's lock clicked.

Nicholas entered the room empty-handed. "I'm glad you're awake. Do you need something?"

"I'm hungry for lunch."

"I'll assist you to the dining room, Miss." His voice, devoid of emotion, led her to worry. *Were the brothers still angry with her because she remembered her name?*

She preferred a tray in her room because of *the incident* but didn't want to rile the brothers. She slipped her hand around Nicholas's arm. He led her to the table where Jameson sat waiting for them. In a quiet huff, she eased into the seat by Nicholas, her eyes studying the table. She couldn't bear to look Jameson in the face. His behavior toward her this morning painted him horrendous in her eyes, regardless of his tastefully covered wounds. Uneasy from the intensity of his gaze, she angled her chair away from him.

"Did you have a restful sleep?" Compassion oozed from his voice.

"I had no choice." How could he show kindness when he'd spoken with such out-of-character firmness earlier? She focused on the rising waves outside the window behind him, refusing to meet his eyes.

He rang a bell on the table.

Esther entered the dining room in her simple sundress topped with a teal apron. "Did you need something, Jameson?"

"Would you bring lunch, please?"

She left the room but returned a few minutes later with filled plates, which she placed on the table.

"Thank you." Sloan picked apart the lettuce, chicken, and shredded veggies, checking for medicine or poison, given the circumstances.

Jameson placed his elbows on the table and studied her endeavor. "Your food is safe, Sloan." He raised a rolled lettuce leaf wrap to his mouth. After swallowing a bite, he added, "See, the food is delicious. Esther added a spicy peanut sauce."

He called her by name. The small victory meant everything to her. She stopped picking at her lunch and glanced up as he finished the wrap and sat back in his chair. "Someday, I'll share why we were so harsh," he said.

There was no reason for him to speak as he had earlier or to relock her room and force her to nap. *Had he never heard of discussions?* "I'd like to go outside and enjoy the beach, the island, anything but this house." And all of you, she wanted to add, but she bit her lip.

Esther appeared at the table and wiped her hands on the apron. "It's windy and rainy outside, but I'd love to take you on a tour of Paradise Island. Time is something I have in abundance."

Going anywhere with the evil cook who had brought her red juice laced with whatever it was to control her mind was out of the question. Sloan refrained from uttering a string of anger-coated words.

"It's okay, Esther," Jameson laced his fingers over his waist and directed his focus at Sloan. "I'll take her for a ride in our carriage."

Sloan raised her glass and sipped the water, trying to divert the enthusiastic chatter threatening to depart from her lips, but it burst out anyway. "When? I want to see everything."

"I'll harness the steeds. Nicholas can give us a relaxing spin around the island. We have umbrellas." Jameson raised an eyebrow at his brother. "That is, if you wouldn't mind."

"I have a few chores to finish, then I'd be happy to do it." Nicholas excused himself from the dining room.

"That settles it." Jameson pushed his plate aside and stood. "We'll leave soon. On our return, we can tour the mansion if you'd like, Sloan." He offered her his arm. "I'll escort you to your room."

Unable to contain her delight another minute, Sloan gushed, "I'd love to see everything." She accepted his arm and floated to her room on wings of happiness. Leaving the house would mark a giant step toward freedom.

Despite the rain, Jameson kept his promise. He brought a carriage to the back door and led Sloan there from her room. "I purchased this 18th-century antique in America and had it shipped here years ago." He held its door open for her.

Sloan inspected the sizable conveyance. The interior was in mint condition with plush, padded walls and seats. Jameson offered her his hand. She stepped inside and spotted a picnic basket with a folded blanket on a bench, forcing her to sit opposite them.

Jameson planted his bottom on the space beside her. "We save this transportation for special occasions. Most often, Nicholas and I go horseback riding or use the cart. It won't be long until you can ride."

Sloan folded her lips, not paying him any mind. She might have desired horseback riding with them, but not now, not after "the nap."

"The carriage is enchanting. I feel like Cinderella attending a ball," she said. It was true, but she didn't mean for her exuberance to slip.

The back door of the mansion opened, and Nicholas sauntered outside. "Ready, brother?"

Jameson glanced at Sloan. She nodded. "We are," he said.

Nicholas climbed to the driver's perch atop the carriage. He snapped the reins, prompting the horses away from the mansion in a direction Sloan hadn't been. The breathtaking beach and waves on her right and the dense jungle with vines and leafy trees on her left stretched for miles.

Before long, the horses left the path. The carriage traveled inland, where fields came into view. Jameson hollered for Nicholas to stop. "Come and join me in the orchard, Sloan." He jumped from the carriage and offered her his hand.

She descended the steps eager to view the plush green land populated with tropical trees—banana, papaya, and citrus fruits. Farther down a dirt road, various tree varieties swayed in the wind. "Your orchards are impressive." Sloan plucked an oversized apple and bit into its firm flesh. "Delicious."

After returning to the carriage, they traveled farther inland to several pastures dotted with cows, sheep, and horses. She spotted barns, silos, several immense vegetable and grain gardens, a pigpen and chicken coops.

"We're self-sufficient here." Jameson expanded his chest with pride. "Esther bakes in the stone ovens behind the mansion. I'm not sure if you've already guessed, but she also cooks and cans vegetables on a wood-burning stove in our kitchen. Speaking of Esther, there's her home." He motioned to a small cottage. "We built the Sims' and Boyds' homes to their specifications. The stone and concrete exterior will survive tropical storms and heat waves. Have you noticed my staff members don't have children? It's their choice."

Jameson pointed to the landscaping in the Sims' yard. Bushes bordered the front and perennial flower beds flourished on the sides of the cottage, which had striped awnings over the windows. "Esther insisted on a small home since she spends most of her days in the mansion, but Herb desires privacy in the evenings. He's our handyman and beekeeper. Plus, he works in the fields."

"The island lives up to its name." Sloan soaked in the incomparable beauty. The natural flora gave the home and its surroundings a sense of peace in every direction.

"I wouldn't sell this island for billions of dollars because of its tranquility." Jameson focused on a home in the distance. "There's Dr. Boyd's residence. Is it familiar? It's up the beach from the mansion. We've made an arc in our travels." Jameson gestured to the quaint cottage. "August Boyd is quite friendly. He works in the gardens and orchards to exercise and chat with staff members, but his medical skills serve us well. He doctored the troops overseas. His expertise is the reason I survived my wounds in the military hospital. Thankfully,

he accepted my offer to relocate to Paradise Island. His wife, Ivy, is my housekeeper. She's the organized type."

The info was interesting, but not as much as learning more about the other survivor. Sloan leaned as far as possible out of the carriage window, trying to see through Dr. Boyd's picture window. "Can we stop by and say hello to them and their guest?" She dropped in her seat and fiddled with the hem of her top. "It's important to me."

"I promise we'll visit soon. But today, I'd like to show you where I go for solitude."

Chapter Thirty-Seven

Twigs crunched and mud puddles splashed under the carriage wheels as they rolled along a rough-hewn road past Dr. Boyd's home. The conveyance veered through a jungle overgrown with vast ferns and vines. Occasional hissing snakes dangled from branches and slithered up tree trunks. Sloan reared away from the window when she spotted them, but Jameson assured her she was safe in the carriage.

Overhead, multicolored tropical birds soared from branch to branch, cawing and chirping as though announcing the brothers' arrival.

Sloan gazed at their breathtaking beauty. "The jungle is astonishing."

"I never tire of it." Jameson pointed to a yellow-bellied Bananaquit bird with a white stripe on the side of its head. "Isn't it beautiful? They usually frequent our floral gardens."

Sloan nodded in answer to his question.

The carriage continued along the dirt path before traveling around a mountain. Nicholas guided the horses to a clearing near a cliff. Before long, he brought them to a gentle halt. After Sloan and Jameson stepped down from the carriage, she limped to the precipice and gazed beyond the jungle at dunes tapering to a shoreline and

sandy beach. Clouds threatened another downpour as waves smacked the sand and retreated like impish pranksters.

Sloan reveled in the magnificent view with Jameson beside her, his arm draped over her shoulder. It was more beautiful than she could have imagined.

"Our favorite place is below the waterfall." He looked down the mountainside. "It spills into a lagoon that's as blue as the most exquisite sapphire. You'll see it below if you stand closer to the precipice."

She stepped to the edge, her toes wiggling over the side. Taking a deep breath, she looked down and gasped. Water rushed toward the bottom, churned, and dispersed into a liquid sapphire lagoon. Every direction presented beauty beyond what Sloan had imagined. She peered into the water at fish darting in schools, their vivid blues, greens, and yellows producing a rainbow of life below the surface. Turtles lounged in the shallows, content to bask in the beauty as white sand framed the pool, creating a perfect sanctuary.

Above the lagoon, birds soared across the sky, heading away from the island. She understood why he loved this place. The beauty never ended. Jameson stood behind her, his soft breath warming her neck. She tilted her head at him, and he smiled. Mixed feelings stirred in Sloan's heart. Before his harsh words this morning, she'd only known the compassionate Jameson whose nature drew her close. His kindness made the eye patch and nose prosthesis invisible in her mind, allowing her to take in his character and not his injuries.

"This place is breathtaking." Sloan meant every word.

She gazed at the beauty for several minutes, admiring the waterfall and listening to the sounds of nature. But the clouds let loose a downpour, forcing them back to the carriage.

Nicholas greeted them from his perch with an umbrella over his head. They hastened into the carriage, sopping wet, but Jameson quickly covered Sloan with the blanket from the opposite seat. Nicholas waited until they settled, then clicked his tongue for the horses to continue their journey. As they wove around the mountain, heading down to the shoreline, the enormity of natural wonders on Paradise Island provided perfect entertainment.

When the carriage reached the beach surrounding the island, Nicholas reined the horses to a stop, and Jameson assisted Sloan from the carriage. "My brother mentioned you've been eager to experience the Caribbean Sea." Jameson led her to the water that lapped the beach.

Sloan couldn't believe how much Jameson had shown her already, and now, wet sand pampered her feet.

He raised an umbrella over her head, protecting her from the last drops of rain, and together, they waded into the sea as its waves crashed at their waistlines. Several yards into the water, Jameson tugged her to turn around. He placed her arms around his neck and settled his free hand on her waist. Gazing deep into her eyes, he brushed his lips over hers. "Am I out of line?" His minty breath coaxed her to give in.

The sweet moment tempted Sloan to yield to his charm, but a sudden jolt snapped her to reality. He had threatened her earlier. "I'm not ready for this." She removed her arms from his neck.

"Is it because of my appearance?" Jameson lowered his forehead to hers.

"It's because I don't understand you, Jameson. You spoke to me harshly this morning and keep me in a locked room. How would you expect me to act?"

Until this morning, she had admired his kindness and overlooked his injuries. She had even dreamed of a relationship, but now, fears invaded her reasoning. Who

was the real Jameson Briggs? The man who desired a romantic moment, yet was capable of intense anger, as Nicholas told her, or the man she'd constructed from the stories Jameson had shared? Those questions distressed her, but many more surfaced, adding to her growing confusion about the mysterious recluse.

Chapter Thirty-Eight

The rain had finally stopped. Jameson stretched from the carriage and tapped the roof. "Take the quick route, Nicholas." His brother veered to a trail leading inland.

"Whoa, boys," Nicholas said to the horses. The carriage halted and he jumped from the driver's perch with a small basket in hand. "Enjoy dinner while I hike the mountain. I'll return to take you home." He jogged away, not looking back.

"Wonderful. It's been a long day, Sloan, but I wanted you to see the island and experience the Caribbean Sea. For dinner, I planned something special." He removed the larger basket from the opposite seat, and Sloan folded the blanket over her arm before he assisted her to the ground.

He led her down a narrow trail through flowering lilies, rose bushes, and dahlias. "This is where I come when my problems are too difficult to bear."

When they arrived at the sapphire lagoon, Sloan's eyes lit up. "It's even more impressive here. The deep blue is more stunning than from the cliff." She studied a turtle sitting on a rock ledge in the water. "What problems could you possibly have on this island, Jameson?"

He spread the thick blanket on the wet sand and sat down on it. "My injuries feel like chains around my heart."

Regret followed him for going back and surprising the guard and for inspecting the bin for plutonium. He had made poor decisions. Decisions that continued to plague him in the dead of night. His body often shook with nightmares, and the emotional and abdominal pain tortured him beyond the ability to cope. "I wonder how much longer I have on this earth?" He laid on his back and crossed his wrists over his eyes. Fighting back the emotions ready to spill, he glanced at the woman beside him who had patiently understood his pain.

She returned his gaze with compassion in her eyes. Her subtle touch on his arm spread warmth through his veins, making his body feel alive from the numbness he'd endured since the accident.

"The distress over what I've lost is unfathomable. I've tried and tried, but I can't let it go."

"It's okay." Sloan's soft voice sounded like that of an angel. "You have a strong jaw, gorgeous hair, and a sweet smile. They make you handsome, Jameson, and your usually charming personality helps me overlook your injuries. You can't go back and change the past, but you can move forward and focus on what's before you. You're stronger than you allow yourself credit."

She was right. It was time to let go of his past and live for the future. He studied the horizon, imagining life without pain or regret. With Sloan's support, he could do anything, be anything he desired. If she were content to live with him on the island, his terrors might fade, and his life might evolve into something special.

Sloan removed his arms from his face. "I just had a memory, Jameson. Plastic surgery has come a long way. They make three-dimensional noses and perform reconstructions. They also make artificial eyes that move with the unaffected eye. No one knows they aren't real. A plastic surgeon can even repair your jagged scar so it'll blend with your face. You could return to the same Jameson you've always been."

"But you don't understand, Sloan. People can be cruel. They make fun of those who are out of the ordinary. People like me. I've had PTSD ever since the accident, but after Veronica screamed and called me 'hideous,' I developed agoraphobia. I don't want to subject myself to ridicule while waiting for surgery. You can't imagine how much my self-concept is damaged."

"I understand." The worry in Sloan's eyes wrapped his fragile soul with concern. "Please consider surgery. Enduring emotional pain until the appointed date might lead to regaining your losses afterward. Wouldn't it be worth the discomfort? I'm sure you and the others could make a small boat and travel to the mainland. I remember someone telling me, 'You can accomplish most things if you're willing to put in the work.'" Sloan became quiet.

"Are you okay?" Jameson asked.

"I'm fine. I was thinking how mysterious you look with the brown eye patch. It radiates an air of intrigue." Sloan found a smooth pebble and rolled it in her hands.

"Would you be disappointed if I don't seek surgery and remain the same?" Jameson sat on the blanket and skipped a stone in the lagoon.

"The surgery might relieve your depression."

"My fear of people is too intense. I'll never leave this island." He walked about thirty feet to an area near the waterfall. "Please join me," he called to her. "I'd like to show you something."

Sloan plucked a wild rose and stroked a smooth petal on her way to the mountain's base. She tossed the flower aside as Jameson helped her climb several wide-based rock ledges.

"See the tributary in the distance?" he asked. "It's a sprout from the Caribbean Sea. If you look carefully, you might spot Old Fella. He's the meanest and most enormous crocodile that ever lived."

She cupped a hand over her eyes. "I don't see him."

"He hides under foliage."

"Are you okay with spending your life without a wife or children?" she asked as they balanced on the ledge.

"I dream of having a family. Maybe someday it'll happen for me." Jameson leaped to the ground and raised his arms for hers. He slipped his hands around her waist and helped her down. Before she stepped away, he brought her to his chest. "You're the most striking woman I've ever met."

"Jameson, I'm still upset with you."

He brushed her soft hair from her face. "Please believe me, there's a good reason why I lock you in your room. It's not from cruelty. If you don't mind, I'd like to change the subject. I've grown to enjoy your company. Maybe some day we can have a deeper relationship."

"As long as I'm a prisoner, it's impossible."

"As I've said, I'll explain everything soon." Jameson lowered his lips to hers.

She pushed him away. "I can't."

Crushed, he released her. "I suppose we should head back to the blanket and eat dinner. It's getting late."

The aromas of roasted quail, cheese, and biscuits filled the air when he opened the basket.

Sloan placed food on her plate but ate in silence. They returned to the carriage soon after to find Nicholas leaning against the conveyance, plucking rose petals. His smile was as big as its wheels. "Did you have a nice outing?" he asked.

"I had a pleasant time with Sloan," Jameson replied.

"But why the grin and sparkle in your eyes, brother?"

"I had a most wonderful afternoon too."

Sloan walked to the dining room and deposited the picnic basket on the table. The day had been long but pleasant. The wind's coolness over her skin, the sea's smells, and the jungle's sounds had satisfied her longing for the outdoors, at least for today.

"I'll give you a house tour, Sloan. But you might drop from fatigue by the time we finish." Jameson draped the wet blanket over a chair.

A screeching noise came from a radio on the buffet. Nicholas adjusted the dial before sitting on a chair at the table.

"Storm Warning! Storm Warning! This is not a watch. Hurricane-force winds are heading toward the western Caribbean islands. A Category 3 storm will make landfall by tomorrow evening."

"Did you hear, Jameson? It's a full-out warning, not an alert." Sloan pulled up a chair by the radio. "Paradise Island is in the hurricane's path."

"I suppose we'll have to head to the storm shelter tomorrow. Are you ready for a tour of the mansion, Sloan?" Jameson placed his hands on his hips and waited for her response.

She was concerned by his lack of urgency regarding the impending storm. Some hurricanes caused significant destruction in the tropics. Memories surfaced often now.

"I'm ready." She walked with him through the home, thankful her foot had held up well during the day with the extra bandages for support. She admired the brothers' relaxed furnishings.

Jameson showed her the four floors and ended the tour by taking her through the kitchen to the lower level. At the far end of a hallway, he entered a solarium filled with tropical plants. A leafy Schefflera tree surrounded by padded benches rose to the ceiling, and six kayaks nested on a rack facing floor-to-ceiling windows. Outside, a patio and dunes led to the beach.

"Do you ever use the kayaks?" Sloan ran her fingers over the lime green one.

"We do, but they're touring kayaks and aren't built for speed or distances, plus their flat bottoms make them difficult to paddle. We should have bought sea kayaks."

He led her through the solarium to the hallway leading to the stairs. Sloan spotted a door Jameson hadn't opened. "What's in there?"

"That's my private room. It's off-limits to everyone, including my staff. Ivy Boyd has strict instructions not to clean in there."

"Would you show it to me? I'm curious."

Jameson's sweet disposition changed to a harsh one. "I can't. Please don't test my limits." His voice escalated as he spoke.

Sloan had no desire to rile his temper. She walked past the room, then waited for him to lead the way. "What are your plans for the hurricane?"

"We'll take it hour by hour. I should have shown you the storm bunker today, but there wasn't enough time." Jameson escorted her up the stairs to the kitchen on the main level.

His failure to begin preparations for the impending storm puzzled Sloan, but his refusal to open the locked room was even more perplexing. *What was hidden in there that he didn't want anyone to see?* She hoped it wasn't Veronica.

Chapter Thirty-Nine

Rob braced against the railing as storm clouds churned faster overhead and ominous waves curled higher and splashed harder against his yacht. Though he doubted his eyes, a tiny dot appeared in the distance—the possibility of land. "Good thing I bought these today." He pulled his rain slicker hood over his head before peering through the binoculars again. "I don't see any buildings, but a cabin cruiser just came into view. I wonder if the owner has info about Sloan and Vivi?" The wind and rain pushed him off balance, but he refused to seek shelter in the yacht's cabin.

Delroy flipped his slicker's hood over his hairless dome, then reached for the binoculars. "We'll need to use our dinghy to visit the cruiser," he said after taking a look.

"Lead the way," Rob said.

The detective lowered the small craft into the water and descended into it from the yacht's ladder. A wave tossed the boat, but Delroy adjusted his weight to maintain balance. "The sea is mighty choppy this evening, boss."

Worried he might fall into the water and become shark food, Rob hesitated to climb aboard until Delroy extended an oar. Rob grasped it for support then dropped into the craft. The detective started the outboard motor and steered the tiller toward the cruiser.

"Did I ever mention the dangerous islands in the Caribbean?" Delroy turned his attention to the island ahead.

"More times than I can count, Detective. But we'll have to take our chances." As they neared the cruiser, Rob's gut twisted into what his uncle called a bow knot—a knot that tightened under more stress. He had to relax. There was no reason for fear—yet. "I hope the island is safe."

"A little late for hope, boss." Delroy focused on the water in his usual go-with-the-flow manner.

Music blasted from the cruiser on their approach.

Delroy dropped anchor by its ladder, and Rob climbed the metal rungs. After reaching the top, he jumped aboard. "Anyone here?" he shouted. The ear-splitting rap music and laughter drowned his words.

He leaned over the cruiser and spotted Delroy struggling to climb. "You coming aboard, Detective?"

Delroy lumbered up the ladder, huffing and puffing, his nostrils flaring. Rob tugged him over the side until he dropped to the deck. Hovering over his face, Rob monitored every breath. "Don't forget your pursed-lip breathing, detective. Whistle. Don't forget to whistle."

"Easy for you to say." His breathing finally eased after several minutes. Rob extended his hand and assisted Delroy up from the deck.

"Let's head to those windows." Rob motioned for him to creep.

Thankfully, the raucous music inside the cabin muted their steps on the creaky deck boards. When they reached the cabin, Rob placed his ear near the window. Easy Joe's raspy voice and Trinidad's deep tone were unmistakable. Rob looked at Delroy. "What are they up to?"

"Good question, boss."

Rob took a quick peek.

He spotted Easy Joe's head. The van driver hacked and wheezed before wiping his mouth with a cloth. "I had a plan for that Rob guy. I was going to hang him over a cliff until someone coughed up some money."

Rob had suspected Easy Joe was up to no good. He recalled the driver sizing him up several times, probably estimating his worth. Rob raised on the balls of his feet until his eyes met the corner of the window. His jaw dropped open.

Five figures scrunched around a built-in table in the center of the room—a man with a red and yellow hat over ginger hair, a man with a tattered cap riding back saddle over scraggly hair, a woman in a lemon-yellow shirt, holding a squirming toddler, a baldheaded man with a gold loop earring and snake tattoos, and a fifth man with a bushy beard, whom Rob didn't recognize.

A news flash hit him. Delroy had taken him to see Kingfish to flesh out a suspect. The detective was much brighter than Rob thought. He focused his attention on the conversation in the cabin.

"Trinidad, we'd be running your scam right now if you hadn't crashed. We can't do nothing with them ladies missing." Kingfish chewed on a toothpick as he dealt playing cards.

"The plane crash ruined everything." Trinidad slumped against the bench, draping his arms over the back. "But somebody named Rob hired Detective Delroy to investigate the crash. I'll be in trouble if they keep snooping around. My plane had violations, and I don't own any insurance." He retrieved a pacifier from the floor. "Good thing Captain Reynauld saved me."

"No problem, Trinidad." The bushy-haired captain studied his cards.

So Captain Reynauld was as devious as the others in the room? Rob had thought something wasn't right about the sea story rescue the man told.

"Plane violations and no insurance are the least of your worries. If the ladies drowned, you'll get manslaughter charges." Easy Joe folded the cards Kingfish dealt him. "Another bad hand." He threw them on the table.

Trinidad rinsed the pacifier under a wet-bar faucet and placed it back in the whining toddler's mouth. "I'll need to lay low until this whole thing blows over. It's a pity because tourists are loaded with money, right? I would've told the ladies my plane needed oil. Would've brought them here. All you guys had to do was offer them a ride to their resort in the cruiser for a few thousand dollars." Trinidad crossed his ankle over his knee and locked his fingers behind his head. "Mac and I need the money to raise our boy." He glanced at the sleeping ginger-haired toddler, pride emanating from his tone.

"Would've been a simple plan." Kingfish stood, edged past the bushy-bearded man, and walked to the coffeepot. He poured the brew into a cup. "Delroy and that Rob guy with him came snooping around my place too. Ain't nobody on Scarlett Bay going to mess with the detective though. He's big as a cement shed and twice as solid." As he sipped the coffee, a scowl interrupted his conversation. "This stuff tastes like engine grease. Who made it?" He looked at the van driver. "You, Joe?"

Easy Joe fiddled with his fingers.

Kingfish tossed the tarry stuff in the sink. "I've got too much on my mind to play cards." He planted his hands on the counter and swiveled his upper torso to view Mac. The snakes on his arms reared their hissing heads at her. "Hey, how about making a fresh pot of Java, girlie?"

"How about making it yourself?" Mac flipped her cards upside down on the table before kissing her boy. "I did my part in the scam, but the ladies wouldn't let me drive them to their resort. I would've collected a hefty sum then and there."

"Well, your plan didn't work, missy, so no use bragging." Griping under his breath, Kingfish emptied the pot's contents in the sink. Once he'd made a fresh brew, he poured a steaming cup. "Ahh, mighty fine." He slid into his seat at the table. "I hate to harp on it, Trinidad, but what will you do about the detective and the other fella?"

Trinidad massaged his temples. "Yesterday, before sunrise, I removed the caulking and cracked a floorboard in the detective's old boat. I thought for sure they'd be goners by now."

Outside on the deck, Rob glanced at Delroy from the corner of his eye. Delroy motioned he would creep under another window to hear better. The wind whipped him as he stood. After a few steps, he tripped over a rope. His body crashed to the deck. Rob cringed as Trinidad hurried to the windows and peered out. The others in the room joined him, and an eerie hush fell over the room.

Every nerve in Rob's body stood at attention. His intuition screamed for him to jump overboard, but fear of the waves and sharks paralyzed him.

"Who are you?" Trinidad glowered at them.

Rob ran his fingers through his messy hair, certain that his scruffy beard and casual attire made him unrecognizable. "We're tourists," he said.

"What are you doing snooping around our boat?" Kingfish narrowed his eyes at Delroy.

Stubble covered the detective's lower scalp, and thick facial hair hid his mouth and jaw. Kingfish didn't indicate he'd recognized him.

"We've got a hurricane heading our way," Delroy said. "We're searching for a place to dock."

"We heard about it on our radio," Kingfish said. "And we would have heard your boat too if Mac's music wasn't so brain-numbing loud." He cocked his head at the taxi driver who ignored his steady glare.

Rob's chest tightened. *What would they do to him and the detective?*

"We'll leave." Delroy flexed his muscles at Rob, showing him to toughen up.

Trinidad's face lit up. "Look out there. They have a yacht." The group exchanged glances before Trinidad grinned. "You're not going anywhere. I can sell that baby for millions."

A chill ran down Rob's spine.

Chapter Forty

After Jameson's tour, Sloan's mind spun with ideas for a new plan. But for now, she had to prepare to leave for the shelter. She dressed in the clothes Nicholas hung in her room this morning—a shoulder-hugging top over a flouncy, calf-length Boho skirt. The clothes looked familiar, but she couldn't remember where she'd seen them. She brushed her long tresses and pulled them into a neck-hugging ponytail.

A hairpin would be necessary for her scheme to work. A drawer in the vanity held hair accessories and makeup. *Had they belonged to Veronica?* She rummaged through the contents and found two bobby pins to secure the wayward strands from her face. Lingering before the mirror, she noticed her chalky skin from confinement in her room. *Hadn't her captors noticed?*

She glanced at her healing foot. Three elastic wraps provided ample support without the poker stick. Now, she had one less thing to hinder her plan.

The door's lock clicked.

Nicholas strolled into the room without a tray. His eyes brightened as she walked from the en suite to the sofa.

"You're beautiful," he said. He'd never paid her compliments. "Would you care to join us for breakfast?"

Except for yesterday's outing, meals outside of her room were the sole activity the brothers allowed her. She had hoped they'd loosen security after yesterday's trip, but they didn't. "I'd like that," she said. Keeping up pretenses, she smiled back at him.

He studied her gait as she walked down the hall. "You're not using the poker this morning."

"My foot feels better." Sloan's limp had improved with the elastic supports.

"Good morning, Sloan." Jameson rose from the table when she and Nicholas rounded the corner to the dining room. He assisted her into a chair.

She appreciated seeing him at breakfast. The valiant Jameson Briggs wasn't as monstrous as he'd led her to believe, but then again, she refused to consider the wounds beneath his prostheses. He deserved for her to treat him better than that.

Appetizing food adorned the table—omelets, roasted potatoes, cubed papaya, sweet rolls topped with chopped nuts and honey, and more. Beyond the windows, gloomy clouds drifted together, covering the sky like a smoldering blanket. Beneath them, trees groaned in the wind, their leaves and branches bowing to the ground.

"The waves are perfect for surfing." A grin spread Jameson's lips as he raised an eyebrow at Nicholas. "We should get our boards and head to the beach."

Were they fools? There was no time to ride skyscraper waves when they needed to prepare for the storm.

"How can you surf with your nose injury?" Sloan asked.

"Ever hear of the expression—where there's a will, there's a way? I found a way to do it," Jameson replied.

"But aren't you concerned about the hurricane?" Sloan filled her plate while eyeing the brothers for traces of insanity.

"Not particularly." Jameson took an extra-long drink from his cup. "We built a cement bunker in the mountainside and stocked it with survival supplies. Fresh food and maybe more batteries and lanterns are all we'll need. If we leave this afternoon, we'll have plenty of time to reach the shelter." He cleaned his plate and excused himself from the table.

Nicholas watched Sloan with the sharp eyes of a hawk as she cleaned her plate. He hopped from his seat when she tossed her napkin on the table. "Ready to return to your room?"

Was she ever ready for that? No. Not wishing to irritate him, she agreed.

Taking lengthy strides, he escorted her to the door but tarried before leaving. "I have to join Jameson. Please don't try to leave. We'll take you to the shelter later." He rushed away after locking the door.

Rather than fretting about the hurricane, Sloan spent the day reading while waiting for the brothers to return. Once in a while, she walked by the window, but as much as she squinted, she couldn't see the brothers' daredevil surfing skills. Bored, she strolled to the mantle and studied the pictures. Jameson and Nicholas had broad smiles in every photo. Judging by their manners, they'd had a wonderful upbringing. She reached for the picture of Jameson and Veronica, but it wasn't there. The brothers had the right to remove any photo, but why the one with Veronica? Sloan returned to the sofa and resumed reading "Emma."

Before long, the dark sky hid the sun, and a knock on the door startled her.

The lock clicked.

Jameson entered the room. "Would you mind helping us latch the shutters?"

Eager to do anything but sit in her room, she helped them with the task. When they finished, she followed

Jameson, who carried a lantern and a bulky burlap sack to the cement barn. "I'll harness Blaze. He's my steed," he said. "We'll take the wagon to the bunker." He entered the structure and walked to a stall. "Our animals are safe in here."

Sloan wandered around while he prepared his steed for the wagon. Clean straw filled the stalls which housed four majestic horses. One nudged her to pet him, and she stroked his shiny hair.

"Would you give them carrots and apples from the bag?" Jameson nodded at the sack he'd hung on a hook.

Sloan divided the contents among the horses, setting aside a portion for Blaze. After Jameson prepared the horse and wagon, she carried the bag back to the mansion. Supplies for the wagon lay by the door. Nicholas added an enormous beverage cooler to the pile.

"I'll see you two later when I bring the others to the shelter." He plodded to the barn, head down against the wind.

Jameson removed two vinyl rain cloaks and two lanterns from the stack. "Looks like it's going to downpour soon." He handed Sloan one of each before clutching his abdomen and falling against the wagon. The items in his hands fell to the ground.

Sloan ran to his side. "What's wrong? What can I do to help?"

Bracing his hand on a wheel, Jameson corrected his posture. His bronzed face appeared pasty. "I'll be fine," he said, but a grimace pinched his brow.

"Is there anything I can get you? Pain medicine? Something to drink?" Sloan gathered the lanterns and Jameson's rain cloak from the ground.

"There's medicine at the shelter. We'd better get moving." He accepted a lantern from her hand and pushed the button on the side. A bright light shone. "These are battery-powered for major storms."

Sloan tossed the cloak over his windblown hair. He helped her load into the wagon the items Nicholas set by the door. A robust wind hurried them along as he climbed to the cart's perch, reached down, and grasped her hand. "It's half a mile to the bunker. We'd better hurry before the storm worsens." He pulled her up beside him.

By the lantern's light, Jameson appeared as striking as the first day he'd slipped through the door in her bedroom. Sloan hadn't noticed until now, but he'd lost some weight. She flipped the cloak over her body, covered her head, and studied him again. He possessed many good qualities, yet some things about him made her shiver—such as how he caught Nicholas's eyes when speaking of Veronica and the screaming at night from somewhere in the mansion. But even worse than those things was the secrecy surrounding the locked room. How could she overlook them? There was something strange about the mysterious Jameson Briggs, and it made her uneasy.

His broad shoulders shielded her from the elements as the horse trotted through the jungle's rough trail. She scooted under his arm when he offered her more protection. Now and then, he brought her hand to his lips and kissed it. How could he be controlling yet gentle and kind? Her emotions fluctuated on a slippery sliding scale. On the positive side, she admired his altruistic behavior in the Marines and could ignore his imperfections. Still, on the opposing side, she disliked his secrecy and inclination toward anger and threats. Could a relationship exist with aspects from both ends of the spectrum? She desired a happy life with someone who loved her, kept no secrets, and possessed an even temperament.

A rut in the dirt path jostled the wagon, interrupting her thoughts. The thick green foliage and lofty trees blocked the wind, allowing a safe, though bumpy, ride. When they arrived at the mountain, Jameson led his horse to a cement shelter he'd made there for the animals. He settled Blaze before he and Sloan carried supplies to the bunker he'd built in the mountainside.

"Come Away with Me" played softly from a CD player as they entered the shelter. Candles flickered around the room, and together with battery-powered lanterns, they provided a dim, dreamy glow. The ambiance carried Sloan away from her fears about the raging storm.

"Who prepared this?" she asked. Had Jameson only pretended to go surfing?

He slipped his hand in hers. "Let's tour the shelter." He led her through the living area, bathroom, and six small bedrooms. The place was as comfortable as a small home.

"What's this?" Sloan spun around when they reached the kitchen/dining area. Food covered a linen cloth draped over a table.

"Snacks to distract us from the hurricane," Jameson said.

The peach-scented candles, sweet music, and homemade bread aroma lent a cozy warmth to the room. What was Jameson up to? No matter how hard he worked for her affection, she'd never forget the locked room. Before she had time to reflect, he took her by the hand and pulled her to his chest. Sure-footed, he swayed with her to the music.

Her knees weakened at his charm, but she came to her senses as she remembered who he was—her captor, not a leading man who would sweep her off her feet.

"I hoped this song would convey how I feel about you, Sloan."

His romantic gesture seemed sincere, but how could she be the love of his life? He hadn't seen an unmarried woman in five years.

The song changed to gentle instrumental music playing in the background. "Would you care for a bite to eat?" Jameson asked in his usual charismatic tone.

As they dined, he shared stories about the Boyds and Sims. When his shoulders relaxed, his warm personality and magnetic presence, regardless of his injuries, captivated Sloan. She'd been through much since washing ashore on Paradise Island, and his pleasing behavior had helped her survive.

The candlelight flickered near his face, diminishing his injuries, yet his smooth pink lips and flowing hair caught her attention. How could she resist this man? He'd assured her he locked the bedroom door for her own good. But what did that mean—her own good? Imprisoning someone wasn't acceptable. Couldn't she decide for herself when to lock her door? Were his words phony coverups to keep her for himself?

He inched so close to her, his lips hovered over hers.

Sloan turned her head, reached for her glass, and downed a sip.

Ignoring her rejection, Jameson discussed the life he wanted to build with her on Paradise Island—a life which included horseback riding, surfing, and starting a family.

"You have wonderful dreams, Jameson." But could she live like this forever—in a remote paradise, wrapped in his charm?

Outside, the wind's rhythmic screeches rattled the door as though attempting to break in. She glanced in its direction, but Jameson's gentle touch of her arm reassured her they were safe inside. "Don't worry, Sloan, we built the bunker with hurricanes in mind." He selected a spatula to cut the dessert. "Would you like some blueberry crisp?" He transferred portions to their plates when she nodded.

She scooped a bite and slipped it into her mouth. "This is delicious." Even though she didn't trust Esther, the lady was a fantastic cook.

Jameson picked at his dessert as Sloan ate. When she finished her last bite, he pushed his plate aside and offered her his hand. "Would you do me the honor?" She rose from her seat, and he tapped the CD player. "At Last" began playing. His muscular arms surrounded hers, and her resolve to remain detached melted again.

As she listened to the song's lyrics, heat traveled up her neck and over her cheeks. The music ended and she studied his lovelorn expression. "I don't know what to say."

"You don't have to say anything. The song expresses how I feel."

Sloan's heart and mind battled over opposing feelings about the enigmatic Jameson Briggs. Even though she'd seen snippets of his bad temper, there didn't appear to be any harm in enjoying this moment with him. He'd been upfront concerning what triggered his anger. Hadn't everyone she'd ever known possessed an internal button that evoked wrath when pushed? Why should she expect perfection from him?

Jameson danced with the smooth steps of a pro, his arms encircled her waist with plenty of room to spare. He was, without a doubt, the most romantic man she'd ever known. As he peered into her eyes, he brought his lips close to hers, but didn't touch them. Sloan felt electricity in the space between them. "I won't kiss you unless you agree," he said.

Her lips neared his, but before they met, she turned her head. The slow song stopped. Faster music began, sparing her an awkward moment. "This song says it all." Jameson twirled her under his arm. "I do get weak when

I'm around you, Sloan. It's hard for me to speak." Jameson danced with her until he dropped on a sofa, laughing.

Sloan sank beside him into the sofa's cushion. He propped his feet on the coffee table and sighed. "This has been the most fun I've had in years."

A knock struck the door.

Nicholas barged into the living room. "Are you two okay, or do you need supervision?"

Jameson's lips twisted as a crimson hue crept over his face. "Bad timing, brother, but I'm glad you're safe."

Esther and Herb walked in behind Nicholas, lugging supplies, including oranges, apples, and vegetables. "Hey, any more music?" Esther asked.

Jameson's steps to the entryway conveyed a lightness throughout the room. "There are tapes in a box by the sofa." He scooped up two bags. "Select whatever you'd like." He helped her carry the supplies to the table.

Joy wasn't Sloan's first thought when she spied Esther, but she couldn't wait for the Boyds to arrive with their guest. Thinking about the other plane survivor triggered an unpleasant memory—Sloan had opened her eyes on a beach without knowing how she'd arrived. Another memory came to mind—a tall, dark-haired man in a doctor's medical jacket. He strode toward her, and his citrus cologne made her swoon. Jameson often wore a similar scent. She felt connected to the man, yet his face remained fuzzy. Had he gone down with the plane? A light-hearted chemistry drew them together. But why couldn't she see his face?

An urgent voice cut her memory short. Jameson spoke into an old-fashioned, battery-powered Walkie-Talkie. "Come in, Doc. This is Jameson. Over."

Sloan bolted from the sofa and joined him while waiting for Doctor Boyd to respond through the device. The storm created static.

FIND ME IN PARADISE

"Shou…we…come…bunker…tonight? Over."

Jameson gripped the device tighter. "Weather's getting worse. We're all here. You decide. Over."

The static continued. "Will…shortly. Over."

If Sloan were alone, she'd sing with joy. She'd soon meet the other survivor.

Chapter Forty-One

The sun had set, casting darkness over the ever-increasing waves. Rob sat with Delroy in the dinghy, and Trinidad barked orders at the detective from the bow. Kingfish, Easy Joe, and Captain Reynauld lowered the cruiser's lifeboat into the water behind them.

The turbulent waves made steering the tiller difficult, but the detective cut through the swells and brought the dinghy alongside Rob's yacht. Trinidad forced Rob and him up the ladder before he clambered aboard behind them.

"Hey, don't I know you two?" He glared at them as they stood on the deck. "You're the guys investigating me. I thought you'd be sleeping with the bottom feeders in the sea by now." The roaring winds and waves striking the boat muted his voice.

"What do you mean?" Rob knew what he meant but wanted Delroy to hear the confession. The wind whipped Rob as his fingernails jabbed his fisted palms.

"Never mind," Trinidad shouted. "I don't know what happened to them ladies you've been ranting about."

A gale blew Trinidad a few yards up the deck. He lowered his head and bore into the wind, trying to return to where he'd left them, but Rob and Delroy seized the opportunity to head to the cabin.

"Where're you two going?" Trinidad shouted.

"Out of the rain," Rob hollered. He wanted as far away from the yacht railing as possible.

Trinidad's gang had arrived on deck, and each of the three possessed enough muscle to heave Rob overboard, unlike the strength needed to overpower the detective. All three thugs would land in the sea alongside him.

Inside the cabin, the air sizzled with tension as Trinidad sat on an armchair squinting at Delroy. *Was he trying to remember the detective's fingers locked around his shirt in the domestic airport?* Delroy had jerked him up from the mattress and brought him so close to their faces Rob could hear Trinidad's labored breathing and smell the bile in his throat.

Trinidad raised both hands. "Listen, maybe we can come to some kind of understanding. The judge won't allow me leniency because law enforcement arrested me too many times. And if the ladies remain missing, he'll try me for manslaughter. I never meant to harm them. I swear it. The crash was an accident. What's the harm in squeezing money from tourists?"

Rob wanted to answer the Harvard grad's question by enlisting Delroy's help to toss him to the sharks, but unlike Trinidad, Rob had a conscience. "Like, what kind of understanding?" he asked. "Where are Sloan and Vivi?"

"Wish I knew." Trinidad removed his soaking-wet Rastafarian hat. "I'm a wanted man, and I don't know what happened to the ladies."

Delroy's face hardened like granite, and his eyes pierced Trinidad's like harpoons. "Ain't our problem. We're taking you in."

Rob glanced at the yacht supplies he'd left on the floor. He'd purchased them during his shopping trip with

Delroy. The rope still laid where Rob had dropped it. His eyes toggled back and forth from it to Delroy several times. He hoped the detective would take the hint.

"Who you planning on taking in?" Kingfish bellowed. He had entered the cabin with Easy Joe and Captain Reynauld in time to hear Delroy's statement.

"We don't have a problem with anyone but Trinidad," Rob replied.

Kingfish glared at both Rob and Delroy as though devising a plan. "How good can you two swim?"

Think, Rob, think. "I had swim lessons in first grade." His answer was pathetic, but what was he supposed to reply under pressure?

"Who cares how good you can swim. It was a rhetorical question." Trinidad copped a menacing sneer. "The way I see it, you two can either jump, or we'll toss you overboard."

Waves. Sharks. Horrible images passed through Rob's mind. Which was worse—the pounding waves drowning them or the sharks eating them? Did it matter? The odds were terrible either way.

"Come on, Delroy, let's jump." Rob walked to the deck's rim alongside the detective. They scanned the water for a few minutes before leaping feet first.

The dinghy had stayed where they'd anchored it. Rob swam to the vessel and climbed aboard. He pulled up the anchor and rowed to Delroy.

The detective gripped the dinghy's side and worked feverishly to haul his lower half into the boat, but neither leg would cooperate. Rob gripped Delroy's pant leg, then his belt, and labored with all his strength to haul him over the side while battling the elements.

"This won't work, boss." Delroy clung to the dinghy, his legs dangling in the water.

"Hold on," Rob shouted over the waves. "I'll maneuver to the yacht's ladder."

Gusty winds and torrential rain partnered to drag them out to sea, but Rob tied a life preserver rope to a handle on the dinghy and placed the ring around Delroy. "Hold on until we reach the ladder, Detective." Employing every ounce of strength he could muster against the deluge striking their faces, Rob rowed the boat. "Hope I can do this before the waves churn us under."

"Hurry, boss."

With fear-induced power, Rob rowed, oblivious to the pain. In record time, he brought Delroy, clinging to the dinghy, alongside the yacht. Delroy grabbed a ladder rung and pulled his body up two steps before dropping into the dinghy. He rolled to his back in the hull, gasping for air.

"We'll use the motor as soon as we're away from the yacht," Rob shouted over the crashing waves. "And we'll stop at the first land mass. I don't care if it is Paradise Island."

Chapter Forty-Two

Roughly thirty minutes later, booming raps struck the bunker door. Sloan double-stepped to keep up with Jameson's long strides to the entry. He swung open the door and stood aside. "Welcome, everyone. I'm glad you're safe."

"I was afraid we wouldn't make it, but the winds aren't as bad as we thought." Dr. Boyd stomped his muddy boots on the doormat and hung his rain gear on a hook.

A plump, gray-haired woman edged around him and scrutinized the room. "Well, hello, dear." She clutched Sloan's hands in hers. "I'm Ivy Boyd. Esther and I cared for you after your unfortunate accident." Her sweet, grandmotherly smile created a relaxed atmosphere.

"Nice to meet you," Sloan said, "but where's your guest—the lady who survived the crash?"

A brunette with wind-blown hair masking her face nudged Ivy aside. "I'm here. I had to chase my scarf. It's nasty out there."

Ivy assisted the lady in removing her rain cloak to accommodate a splint covering her right arm. The young lady's espresso hair tumbled below her shoulders.

Sloan had seen the lady in her dreams but couldn't remember her name.

Using her able arm, the young lady hung her cloak on a hook and winked at Nicholas. He pecked her lips as she ran her hand over his stubbled jaw. Sloan did a double-take. Who was the woman?

The brunette wiped long hair strands from her face. "I'm so glad you're okay, Sloan. Don't you recognize me?"

"I–I–I can't recall your name," Sloan said.

"I'm Vivi, your sister. Do you remember floating on cushions in the sea with me after the plane crashed?"

"Vivi!" Sloan wrapped her in an enormous hug, reluctant to let go. "I remember now. I'm so glad you're okay."

"Do you recall a man in a boat rescuing Trinidad and leaving us stranded in the sea after the plane crashed? I swam us to shore on the plane's floatation pads, then I pulled you up the beach and crawled for help. Hours after I collapsed on the sand, Nicholas found me. He brought me to the Boyd's home in his horse-drawn wagon."

Sloan's skin prickled with goosebumps. "Yes, Vivi, I remember what happened now." She pulled her sister in for another embrace and spun her around. "I can't believe it's you."

"I've waited so long to see you. Dr. Boyd was afraid the swelling in your brain might worsen."

"I'm healed, Viv." Sloan examined her sister at arm's length. "You look healthy."

"It's the sun and island-grown food." Vivi pressed her cheek to Sloan's. "I'm so happy you're well. I'll have the splint removed from my arm before long."

Jameson strolled to Esther's side. "Would you mind serving the hot tea now?"

"Oh, my, yes." Esther walked to the table.

Jameson rummaged through her supplies to find the mugs. He set them on the table next to an insulated beverage jug. Esther filled them with a golden liquid.

"This is just what we need." Dr. Boyd selected a mug and held the brew under his nose. "Hmm. Fresh honey apple cinnamon."

"How about selecting another CD, Esther?" Jameson sipped her tea blend and smiled. "Delicious."

When Esther finished pouring duties, she strode to the CD box and popped a disc into the simple machine. "Here's a good one. I've always loved it. 'Can't Help Falling in Love.'"

The moment Esther clasped Herb's hand, he twirled her under his arm. They snuggled cheek to cheek while dancing to the music.

"Shall we?" Dr. Boyd bowed to his wife. "It's been a while, my dear, but one never forgets the memorable things in life. Do you recall our prom?"

"Indeed, I do, Auggie. You were the handsomest young man there. And I also recall your wild hair." She broke into a loving chuckle as he scratched the sparse hair on his head.

He slipped his hand in hers and spun her around before holding her close to his chest like an infatuated teen.

"Come on, Vivi. We can't let them outdo us." Nicholas helped her stand.

She nuzzled her face in his hair, and he wrapped her in his arms, a little too snug from Sloan's perspective. They behaved like...like...they loved each other.

Jameson set his cup on the table and offered Sloan his hand. "Would you mind another dance?"

She had more important things to consider rather than dancing. Was Vivi naïve to Nicholas's charms? Didn't she know the brothers kept her sister in a locked room?

Sloan reminded herself not to upset the evening because of Jameson's temper. She accepted his invitation even though she longed to speak with her sister.

Jameson lifted Sloan's chin. "I hope you'll be mine forever."

Sloan wished her emotions would stop running hot and cold. One minute, she imagined spending her life with him, but the next, she planned an escape. When the song ended, she headed to the sofa.

Jameson eased down beside her and whispered, "What're you thinking about?"

"I'm enjoying the laughter and music." She couldn't tell Jameson her true thoughts—that she wanted to reminisce with her sister and be free of her locked room.

Esther flitted to the table like a young girl at a high school dance. "Would anyone care for dessert?" She removed the garnet-red dishcloth covering a Dutch apple pie.

"Of course," came the unanimous reply.

After eating, Dr. Boyd turned on the radio. The weary group listened to the newest storm warnings.

"Earlier this evening, the weather report said the winds might fizzle after midnight. They haven't been stronger than a Category 2 storm," Nicholas said.

"Yes, I heard it wouldn't reach a Category 3 as predicted," Dr. Boyd added.

The weatherman proved them right by announcing the worst of the storm had passed and would continue to subside after midnight.

Sloan fidgeted with her shirt. *Would she have enough time after midnight to accomplish her plan before anyone noticed her missing?*

Chapter Forty-Three

Esther kept the warm tea coming, and the cinnamon aroma infused the bunker as Sloan and the others relaxed on the sofas and chairs until 10:00 p.m.

Each time Jameson walked outside to check the storm, Sloan stood in the entryway, viewing the wind and rain. The powerful gusts had dwindled, giving her hope she might slip away to the mansion after bedtime.

When they returned to the living room, she stole Jameson's seat beside Vivi, and he slid down next to Nicholas. The Boyds and Sims engaged in animated chatter as Vivi asked Sloan, "Has your full memory returned, sis?"

"Maybe." Sloan curled against Vivi on the sofa. "I remember drinking hot chocolate in our pajamas when we were younger."

"I remember it too. We sat at the table, and our dad asked if we wanted more. Those days on the farm planted long-lasting memories." Vivi said.

"We had fun growing up in Marysville, didn't we? Do you remember playing with Saige Westbrook on her farm? She lived down the road from us. Now, we work for her and her husband, Gray, in their cardiology clinic. What about Rob? Do you remember him?"

Sloan thought for a moment. *Was he the vague male figure who had appeared in her memories?* The one whose face remained cloudy? "Describe him for me, Viv."

"Let's see. He's tall with stylish dark wavy hair and the most infectious laugh. Do you remember him organizing our clinic vacation? Our coworkers who stayed behind to run the clinic planned to join us in Scarlett Bay for the weekend. You were so worried about Rob missing the flight that we had to take Trinidad's puddle jumper to the resort so you could call him quickly."

"Didn't I bring my cell phone?" Sloan asked.

"You lost it."

Jameson's delighted disposition before his staff arrived plunged into a chin-dragging mope during Vivi's banter with Sloan. He rose from the sofa's arm and paced behind Vivi.

"The more you mention, the more I remember." Sloan wrapped her arms around her knees. "Tell me more."

"Do you recall a wave washing us to shore?" Vivi asked.

"A white plane sank in the sea when we spotted you on the beach." Jameson's blood-red face appeared ready to explode. "Later, Nicholas found Vivi on the sand farther up the beach, and he carted her to Dr. Boyd's house."

"We were flying in Trinidad's puddle jumper, Sloan." Vivi's breathing quickened as she spoke. "It was missing side doors. The engine coughed out smoke, and Trinidad lost control of the plane."

Jameson stood and sidled up to Nicholas, who'd left his spot and stood by Vivi at the end of the sofa. "Let's not encourage Sloan's memories, brother. She might insist on leaving the island."

Sloan overheard the whispers but had bad news for the brothers. Her memory had returned big time, and she wanted her previous life back—clinic work, Dr. Rob, and the rest. But she'd keep the info under wraps until necessary.

"Attention, everyone." Jameson had walked to the center of the room. "It's time we head to bed to conserve candlelight and batteries. Let's enjoy our last cup of tea. Thank you for the delicious treats, Mrs. Sims." He walked to the dining room and slipped his arm around her shoulders in a side-to-side hug.

"What's wrong, Jameson?" she said. "You never call me 'Mrs. Sims' unless you're upset."

"It's nothing." His face grew beefy red as he placed cups in the sink. After doing so, he walked to the CD player and stopped the music. "I hope everyone had a nice evening."

"I enjoyed it." Sloan rose from the sofa. The flip side of Jameson's charm had reared its ugly head. He was treading water in secrecy and manipulation. One last sip emptied her cup. "I'm heading to bed, Viv. Would you like to sleep in my room so we can chat?"

Jameson stepped between them. "Everyone has a private room except for married couples." He polished off his drink. "Your room is down the hall, Sloan. And Vivi's is the first on the right. Everyone should get a good night's sleep. We'll have to remove storm debris from the beach tomorrow."

Sloan walked to her room and shut the door. She couldn't understand Jameson Briggs. He drove her mad with confusion. How could he enchant her one minute and cause fear and dread the next? She imagined him as the handsome Marine in the photo, dressed in military fatigues with close-cropped hair. Today, he had gorgeous, thick hair flowing over his shoulders. He wasn't perfect. She couldn't expect it after all he'd been through. But he wanted something she couldn't give him—a desire to remain on the island.

She scanned her tiny quarters, which had no windows. They were in a bunker chiseled into the mountain. Hand-painted nature scenes decorated the walls, and the quilt on the bed had been hand sewn. On the nightstand someone had placed a book—*The Castaway*. Sloan wasn't sure whether to grin or grimace. Whoever had laid it there possessed a wry sense of humor.

She turned her attention to her plight—the great escape—and more importantly, the uncovering of secrets first. But how could she leave the shelter undetected? It only had one exit—through the front door. Regardless, tonight Sloan hoped to learn the contents of Jameson's secret room.

Unable to sleep, she lay on her bed, waiting for the storm to pass. The hours crawled by as memories flooded her mind. They drifted to Marysville, the clinic, and Rob. She remembered him. He was handsome and had a cute laugh. His calm, sincere, and often playful demeanor had captured her heart. *Would she ever see him again?* She recalled walking through St. Anne's airport with him. They were heading to the Caribbean. She tried to tell him her feelings before leaving on the plane, but an ill-timed phone call stopped her. Why had Rob stayed behind? Had he thought she didn't want to go on a trip with him? Nothing was further from the truth.

She rose from her bed and tiptoed to the door. After opening it, she glanced both ways down the hall and listened for noise.

A dark void stared back until moans and groans broke the silence. Jameson was in pain and needed medicine. Should she find it for him? No. Dr. Boyd or Nicholas would tend to him. She had to reach the mansion.

She tiptoed from her bedroom, carrying the nightstand lantern, and opened Vivi's door. "Are you awake?" she whispered.

Vivi raised her head. "I can't sleep."

"Come with me to the mansion."

"Why?"

"Just come."

Chapter Forty-Four

S loan stood by as Vivi hurried from her bed and changed clothes. Together, they walked to the living area. Afraid of waking the others, Sloan trembled while opening the entry door. The wind still howled, breaking branches and hurling them on the path. Sloan and Vivi closed the door.

The weatherman on the radio had predicted the storm would let up after midnight, and it was only ten. She and Vivi would have to wait. They returned to Sloan's room and curled on the bed. Moans echoed from the hallway. After a lengthy period of imagining the terrors Jameson dreamed behind his door, Sloan abandoned the need for sleep. "Let's go." She whispered in Vivi's ear.

Groggy, Vivi followed her to the bunker's entrance, and Sloan opened the door. As predicted, the wind no longer roared. Salt and fish odors replaced the floral scents outside.

While helping Vivi with her cloak, Sloan worried the brothers would find them gone. The last time she'd gone missing, they doubled their efforts to prevent another escape. What would they do this time?

A strong feeling for Rob rushed over her. She loved him, but her reclusive captor had also woven his charm through her heart. She had to accomplish her plan—unearth the secret he kept in his forbidden room. Above all else, she hoped it wasn't Veronica. Thoughts of what she might find made her shudder. No one locked a room unless it contained something of importance.

Sloan slipped her cloak's hood over her head and stepped outside on the trail with her sister, lantern in hand. Downed trees, broken branches, and foliage littered their path. Vivi matched her strides as wind and rain battered them from the starless sky.

"Why are we heading to the mansion in the middle of the night?" Vivi yawned and pinched her cloak around her neck.

"I'll explain when we get there. Let's hurry." Sloan dodged downed trees, twigs, and branches. "Be careful where you walk, Viv."

The long trek and poor sleep drained Sloan's energy, but they reached the mansion and found it unlocked. Her lantern provided light for them to slip inside. They passed through the entryway and walked to the kitchen.

Sloan's heart pounded so loud in her ears, she couldn't hear Vivi ask, "Is everything okay?"

Vivi asked again and Sloan nodded. She rounded the corner from the kitchen and approached the steps leading to the lower level. Their surroundings, lit by the lantern's glow, proved no one had followed them. Still, Sloan's hands shook as she descended the stairs with her injured foot supported by the tight elastic bandages applied that morning. She stepped lower and lower, Vivi breathing down her neck.

Would Jameson's secrets cause Sloan to admire him less?

Another step down. And another, Sloan slid her hand along the handrail. Lower and lower she went until her foot touched the tiled floor. The lantern showed the way as fear tightened her lungs. She gasped for a deep breath.

"Did you hear a man's voice?" she whispered. "Or was it the wind?"

Vivi shook her head.

The lantern cast a shadow over the solarium at the end of the hallway. The locked door was on Sloan's right. She removed a hairpin from her hair, tiptoed to the forbidden room, and handed the lantern to Vivi, who placed it by the lock to illuminate the keyhole.

In the dead quiet, wet rubber soles squished down each stairstep. Sloan's hand quivered midair.

Vivi turned off the lantern.

Was it Jameson?

Sloan's respirations increased until crushing fear nearly snuffed her breath. He had warned her not to enter the room, and Nicholas had warned her not to flare his temper. Had Jameson followed them?

She and Viv crouched by the door. Careful not to make a sound, Sloan felt for the turning mechanism in the keyhole. Working without light, she located the metal groove and turned it with the hairpin.

Click.

Success.

She twisted the knob, pulled Vivi behind her into the inky darkness, and locked the door. Blinking red and green lights stunned Sloan.

The rubber soles headed down the hall toward them.

Sloan placed a finger over her lips and gripped Vivi's shoulder. After the steps passed the forbidden room, Sloan exhaled.

The footsteps returned. Sloan sucked another breath and held it.

The doorknob jiggled.

Her lungs burned.

The steps squished to the stairs, ascended them, and disappeared.

Sloan needed to return to the bunker before Jameson reached it. But she'd come this far. She had to inspect the room.

Chapter Forty-Five

Fear wrapped its unmerciful arms around Rob's chest and squeezed the air from his lungs as the waves carried the dinghy higher and higher before crashing it into the sea below. "We might not make it, Detective."

"Hang on, boss." Delroy panted, his breathing jagged. "The. Wind. Is slowing. Look up ahead! There's a light." He stared at the coastline.

Rob studied the glow, but it disappeared. "Hurry, Delroy."

Steering the boat away from the curls, Delroy maneuvered the tiller so that the dinghy rode the waves to shore. Rain pelted them as they clambered from the boat and dragged it to the sand. In every direction, palm branches littered the beach. A wind gust selected an extra-big branch and hurled it at Rob.

Delroy raised his hand and deflected the palm leaves flying at his face. "This could be Paradise Island, boss. And you know what that means."

"Perhaps. But for now, I'll choose Marines over sharks." Rob dropped to the wet sand.

"Didn't I tell you? Sharks swim to deeper water during hurricanes," Delroy said.

"Why didn't you tell me that when I was trying to save your life?" Rob pulled seaweed from his hair and tossed it on Delroy's bald head.

The detective removed it and flicked it on the sand. "Not knowing sharks' behavior gave you the strength to row faster, didn't it?" He plunked on the sand beside Rob. "I hate to say it, but this island might be worse than sharks."

"It doesn't matter, Detective. I'm done." Rain sputtered from Rob's mouth as he spoke.

"Me too, boss. I need sleep."

"Exhaustion is only part of it." Rob flopped his arms over his head and stretched on the sand, allowing the rain to cleanse his clothing. "I dislike admitting it, but too many obstacles have hindered our search for Sloan and Vivi, including dangerous islands. The search might kill us. We'll alert the authorities about Trinidad and his gang and let them take over."

"Boss, your fatigue is getting to you. Are you willing to forsake your second chance at love?"

"I'd give my life for Sloan, but if I die, who will search for her? You've been right all along. There's not a chance in the world we'll find her. Seven thousand islands, Detective. Seven thousand opportunities for criminals, druggies, and fanatical ex-military to kidnap or kill her or us." Rob wiped the rain from his face. "I hate to admit it, but I'm done."

"We'll see how you feel in the morning. As far as I'm concerned, we've just begun. I won't let you stop. I give you my word." Delroy lowered his back to the sand where the rain had dug a trench around him. "Somehow, we need to recover your yacht."

"We'll see it again," Rob said, dangling the keys. "Those scammers aren't going anywhere."

Delroy planted his tongue firmly in his cheek. "You're naïve for a surgeon, boss. Ever hear of hot-wiring?"

"Of course. But I lack a criminal mind, Detective. Wait. There's the light you saw! Perhaps we can weather the storm there."

"Whoa. I'm done moving." The detective didn't budge. "The rain is massaging my aching bones."

Rob leaned back on his elbows, then raised his palm to catch the drops. "It's letting up, and we need to keep moving."

Delroy grunted as Rob hopped up and trained his eyes on the light in the distance. "Maybe Sloan and Vivi are there," Rob said.

"Type A personality," Delroy mumbled. He groaned as he pushed to a sitting position and stood.

Waves crashed the beach, and sand shifted beneath their feet, but they trudged up the shoreline.

"What's that?" Rob aimed his finger down the beach.

"I'm not psychic, boss."

"Let's hurry." Rob ran full speed along the shoreline, leaving the detective behind as a multistory house appeared beyond the next dune.

The rain and wind diminished as Rob neared the shelter. *Who would live in such an enormous place? Druggies or fanatical ex-military, like Delroy said?*

He reached the building's door and knocked. "No answer, Detective," he hollered up the beach.

Delroy placed his hands on his thighs, struggling to catch his breath.

"The occupants might have gone to a storm haven. I'm going inside," Rob shouted again.

A mouthwatering aroma lured him into the home—yeasty, buttery, baked bread. Judging by the hearty aroma, the owner hadn't been gone long unless he was still in the home. "Anyone here?" Rob called. The ear-bursting thump-thump of his heart masked further sounds.

He felt along the wall in the darkness and found electrical switches that didn't work. Perhaps wires had been downed by the storm.

A shuffling sound startled him. "Is anyone home?" he shouted again. Arms outstretched, he walked into the unknown. A remote noise reached his ears. *Footsteps? Were they real or the groaning of a home battered by winds?*

He headed in their direction and smacked into something hard, face-first. He rubbed his forehead. Cupboards? His mouth salivated from the tantalizing bread aroma originating in the room. A rail to the left led to steps. He descended them, groping the handrail. The downstairs was several degrees darker than the upstairs. His fingers traced a door frame on his right. He walked the hallway, touching each door. At the end of the hall, he entered an open room.

Leaves brushed his face. Plants.

Careful not to arouse anyone and suffer dire consequences, he returned to the hallway and turned each doorknob. They were locked.

A creaking sound on the upper level startled him. He tiptoed up the stairs and whispered, "Delroy?" The detective closed the kitchen door where he and Rob had entered the home. "Shh," Rob said. "I heard a noise downstairs. It could have been the house settling or the wind tossing branches, but stay alert, Detective."

He and Delroy fumbled through the cupboard area, past a room defined by a table and chairs, and on to an open space. His hands detected armchairs and sofas.

Delroy yawned and rubbed his eyes. "I need to drop. I can't stay this beautiful without sleep. Besides, if I don't get a solid ten, I can't do anything with my hair."

Rob chuckled at the baldheaded detective's joke.

"You a late sleeper, boss?"

"Nah. I'm at the hospital by six most weekdays."

"Sorry, boss. I mean it. I feel for you." The detective collapsed on a sofa and began snoring.

Rob stretched his weary limbs on a separate sofa near Delroy's roost. In the darkness, he listened to the light rain tapping the windows. The winds had stopped. He relaxed for the first time in days, knowing the detective wouldn't allow him to give up on Sloan.

If only she and Vivi had been inside this house.

Chapter Forty-Six

Hoping the footsteps were gone, Sloan turned the lantern on high inside Jameson's forbidden room. A gasp stole her breath away. Vivi slapped her hand over Sloan's gaping mouth.

Computers with nine gigantic screens occupied one entire side wall. Each displayed Caribbean channels or ones from around the world—weather, news, stocks, sports, Caribbean police, world police, and more. Why had Jameson lied? He could have notified the authorities about the plane crash and learned her identity. Those were the operative words—he could have. Instead, he locked her in a room, not wanting her discovered. But why? At this moment, she despised Jameson Briggs. She clenched her fists. He could have taken her to a hospital, but no, he jeopardized her life instead.

"Did you know about this, Viv?"

"They said there wasn't any outside communication. I'm shocked. Why would they hide this?"

"Yeah, and why would they have electricity in this room but nowhere else on the island?" Sloan glanced over her shoulder to make sure no one followed them. "Jameson Briggs is a liar."

Sneaking like thieves, she and Vivi tiptoed past the long computer desk and spotted a door. Sloan gulped.

Her knees wobbled like gelatin. Was Veronica locked in there? Sloan's pounding heart nearly ripped open her chest. She pressed a fist over her mouth before opening the door.

It led outside.

Sloan released her breath. There wasn't another room, and Veronica was nowhere in sight. *Would she have been alive if they'd found her?*

Sloan walked through the door into the rain and wind and found the unexpected— a shiny chopper on a helicopter pad. "How dare Jameson tell me there was no way off this island."

Vivi pushed past Sloan and stared at the chopper. "This is incredible."

Sloan's face burned with anger as she marched past the sleek black aircraft and climbed a dune. The churning sea lay past the beach. But on her left..."Vivi, you've got to see this. You're not going to believe it!"

Steps led from the dune to a covered dock housing a massive yacht. Sloan clamped her teeth to keep from screaming, "Why did Jameson keep us prisoners on this island? Wait, did Nicholas know the truth?"

Vivi shook her head. "He would have told me if he did."

"Let's hurry to the yacht." Sloan raced her sister down the numerous wooden steps.

She reached the vessel first and climbed aboard. Standing on the deck, she gawped at the lavish elegance—designer everything. Where was the navigation room? She'd never been on a yacht but had seen boat captains in movies steering from a room with wraparound windows. On a hunch, she dashed upstairs and burst into the room. It was indeed the steering room. The boat was their way off the island. She rushed from the room and called over the railing, "Help me find the keys, Viv."

Vivi joined her and they searched the entire boat without success.

"Maybe we'll find them in the forbidden room." It was worth a look. Sloan charged up the dune's steps.

Vivi followed her.

The red, yellow, and green computer lights flashed when they opened the door. "Let's notify the police before searching for the keys." Sloan sank into a padded swivel chair and tried logging on a computer. Password screens popped up when she pressed enter. "Oh, this is great. What are Jameson's passwords?"

She tried combinations of Paradise Island, Nicholas, Jameson, and staff names without success. "This is hopeless. We'll never guess the passwords. Let's search for the keys."

Vivi stood off to the side while Sloan rummaged through desk drawers, overhead cubby holes, and behind computer screens, but instead of keys, she found the missing photo from her room—Jameson hugging Veronica. "He seems to have difficulty forgetting the people he loved." She replaced the photo on the desk and looked at Vivi. "Why aren't you helping?"

"I have to tell you something." Vivi fidgeted before leaning against the desk. "I'm not leaving the island."

"Wh–what?" Sloan stammered. "Even after you've learned the truth about communication and transportation? We're prisoners. They deceived us."

"I love Nicholas, and I'm staying."

Sloan clutched Vivi's arms. "You can't mean it. Haven't you heard of Stockholm Syndrome? It's when prisoners begin feeling comfortable with their captors and form relationships. They delude themselves into believing the captors' actions are noble, and they even help them—just to gain their favor. You've known Nicholas for a short time. And he's lied to you. If he loves you, why would he lie?" How could Sloan reason with a starry-eyed woman in love? "Listen, Viv, how does he know what he wants? He hasn't met another woman in five years. And you're leaping into isolation on a remote island. Granted, it's beautiful, but think about it. If he loves you, he'll leave the island with you."

"Sloan, I haven't met anyone as affectionate and compassionate as Nicholas. You'll never change my mind. Dr. Boyd will marry us. He has credentials. Please don't ruin this for us."

"We'll discuss it later. We need to return to the bunker before anyone learns our whereabouts." By anyone, Sloan meant Jameson. *Was it his footsteps she'd heard?*

She and Vivi hurried from the room and tiptoed up the steps to avoid alerting him if he was in the house. Thoughts of impending disaster frightened Sloan. *What would Jameson do if he found her here?* She glanced out the kitchen window. The clouds had lightened. Waves no longer battered the shore.

Raised with adversity, Sloan knew hope could triumph even in horrible circumstances. Her parents had died in a plane crash, leaving her and Vivi orphans when they were young teens. A couple with open arms, whom they now called Mom and Dad, adopted them and turned their lives around. The Briggs brothers holding them prisoner on Paradise Island was yet another adversity, but Sloan planned to overcome it. Jameson had met his match.

After they crept from the mansion, Sloan had an idea. "I have something to do before going to the bunker. I'll catch up with you soon."

Vivi headed to the trail, but Sloan walked to the beach. Sea water surged around her legs as she gathered broken palm branches scattered by the wind and set to work. The sun peeked over the horizon, allowing her light for her task. She had to move fast before the person in the mansion or those in the bunker discovered their absence. After spelling HELP on the sand in gigantic letters, she stepped back to inspect her work. Someone at a distance—in a plane or on a boat out to sea—might recognize the word, but up close, it resembled messy debris from the storm.

Aided by the dawning light, she marched toward the jungle path leading to the bunker.

Chapter Forty-Seven

Halfway up the trail, leaves crunched and twigs cracked. Sloan stood still and listened. Was someone following her? Not a soul shared the path except for chirping tree frogs and crickets. She took a step but stumbled over a log and fell to the ground.

Quickly scanning the surroundings, she froze. An enormous crocodile, at least four times her size, thrust its tail side to side as it sprawled over the path ahead. Tangled vines, bushes, foliage, and trees lining the trail prevented her from escaping into the jungle.

The creature's beady eyes locked on hers. She feared moving or even breathing. How could she escape without losing her life? If she ran, the massive crocodile might find her entertaining prey and accept the challenge. She searched the ground for something to use as a weapon.

A huge rock lay in the dirt beside her.

Using slow movements, she dislodged it. The boulder was larger than a human head.

An idea came to her, and it was worth a try.

The gigantic reptile swished its tail and lumbered toward her as she lay on the ground. If she kicked it, the beast could bite her legs. But she had a better plan. Her movements had to be intentional, not the wild reactions of someone panicking for her life. She had to wait for the right opportunity or lose her chance to stop the creature. One false move and the crocodile would eat her whole.

Shaking, she waited for the beast to make its next move. The cunning creature thrust its tail side to side and studied her with intense eyes.

Sloan prepared to deliver her plan—it wasn't to hit the crocodile on the head and daze it, or worse yet, anger it and cause the creature to seek revenge. No. She had a much better idea.

The crocodile's evil eyes held steady as Sloan's rain cloak swished when she curled her legs. The noise startled the creature, and it opened its enormous jaw, ready to strike. Within seconds, it lurched at her legs, and its mouth snapped shut, missing her by inches.

Her hands shook uncontrollably. *Could she follow through?*

She inched backward, crab-style, then raised the boulder over her head. The crocodile opened its jaw again. This time, he moved closer and leveled his teeth at her feet. Vivi's pink shoe lay in its mouth. Shaking, Sloan screamed, and in one swift burst of anger, she thrust the rock down its throat and fell to her back.

A gunshot rang out and a smoking hole lay between the creature's eyes. Sloan cowered in fright. More shots followed until the crocodile no longer moved.

"Sloan, what are you doing out here?" A figure with broad shoulders ran to where she'd crashed. "You could've been killed." The man scooped her from the ground into his strong arms.

"Is she okay?" Nicholas sprinted to his brother's side.

"Yes, but if we'd arrived a second later, Old Fella would have finished her."

"Where's Vivi?" Nicholas looked both ways. "Did she come too? She's not at the bunker."

"I–I don't know where Viv is. She started back to the bunker before me." Sloan broke down and sobbed, unable to stop. How did her sister's shoe get in Old Fella's mouth?

A light rain fell, and the wind slowed as Sloan, Jameson, and Nicolas trekked through the jungle trail. Broken tree branches and jungle debris slowed their journey.

Her sister had won marathon medals, so reaching the bunker in record time would have been easy. Sloan refused to think otherwise. "Vivi would've found a way to safety."

Nicholas paced the trail. "How much lead time did she have on you?"

"She left about fifteen minutes before me," Sloan said. "But I saw her shoe in Old Fella's mouth." Her lips quivered and she crumpled to the ground as the shock took hold.

Jameson slapped her cheeks. "Open your eyes, Sloan. You'll be okay. We'll find Vivi." He sounded every bit as frightened as Nicholas. "You're strong and so is your sister."

Sloan appreciated the brothers' concerns, but their fear had compounded hers. Had they experienced an event with Old Fella in the past?

"I found another shoe!" Nicholas shouted. He waved a pink slip-on identical to the other shoe. "This proves Vivi was on the path."

"Crocodiles have a reputation for their speed. If Old Fella chased her, she wouldn't have made it far." Jameson scanned the foliage along the trail.

"Old Fella must have startled her. How else would she lose a shoe?" The thought of Vivi falling and Old Fella overtaking her was too much for Sloan to bear. "I–I can't continue. I have to return to the mansion."

Chapter Forty-Eight

R ob rose from the sofa belonging to the enormous house where he and Delroy had stayed the night. "Detective, it's time to get up."

"Is it noon yet?" Delroy groaned.

"No, but we need to leave." He nudged the detective's arm. "The homeowner might return soon."

He raked the unruly hair from his forehead and meandered to the kitchen. So this was where he'd gone last night in the utter darkness. As he spotted the handrail leading to the lower level beyond the cupboards, a robust coffee aroma drifted under his nose. Rob needed a powerful caffeine jolt to awaken his exhausted brain. "Hey, you brewing a pot already?" he asked Delroy.

"Yeah, on a wood-burning stove in an old-fashioned coffee percolator. I thought you might leave some money behind for the owner," Delroy said.

"Sure thing. See if you can rustle up some breakfast too."

"Will do, boss."

On his trip downstairs, Rob spotted a door ajar in the hallway. If memory served him, it wouldn't open last night. Afraid of meeting an angry homeowner, he tiptoed up the stairs. "Let's take the coffee and whatever you found to eat and leave, Detective."

He placed three damp one-hundred-dollar bills on the kitchen counter. "This should cover our overnight stay plus food."

"Right, boss." Delroy loaded a few supplies into a bag before finding a coffee thermos. "We'll have enough to eat for a few hours."

"Good. Let's head back to the dinghy."

The fierce winds last night had reduced to a mere tropical storm, but it left behind branches, twigs, and foliage strewn over the sand. Rob considered gathering the debris as an additional thank you from him and Delroy. "Will you help me, Detective?"

"Nah, boss. They'll want to see what the storm did. Besides, I ain't got enough air left in me to do any work. Let's scram in case this is Paradise Island." Delroy sucked in a breath and blew out a steady whistle.

Rob had hoped the detective's breathing would improve after he rested, but they hadn't slept long. "I get your point, but I don't see Marines storming the beach."

"I wouldn't expect it after a hurricane, boss."

The dinghy lay on the sand where Rob and Delroy had dragged it in the wee hours last night. The storm had deposited additional jungle debris and sea creatures in the hull. Rob removed them while Delroy sat on the sand and sipped coffee from the thermos.

"Let's head out." Rob shoved the boat into shallow water, and Delroy climbed in. After guiding the dinghy farther into the sea, Rob hauled his legs over the side. "I'm sad we didn't find Sloan and Vivi, but if angry ex-military live here, perhaps we shouldn't stir their dander." He paddled away from the island using the oars.

"Are we heading to report Trinidad and his gang in Scarlett Bay?" Delroy sat beside the motor and prepared to steer the tiller.

"Yes, indeed. I hope the police find Sloan and Vivi and return my yacht."

He glanced back at the island. "Wait a minute. Those branches on the sand spell something!"

Delroy cupped his eyes. "It could be I E L ᴼ. Why would someone write hello?"

"Exactly, but there aren't two Ls. The storm must have scattered the letters. Let's figure this out...something...I E L ᴼ."

"Look at the O, boss. It's smaller and higher than the other letters. Maybe it's a P."

"E L P. Delroy, the person tried to spell HELP. I'm sure of it."

Chapter Forty-Nine

Drenched by a fresh round of lighter rain and wind, Sloan returned to the mansion with Jameson and Nicholas. Nicholas walked to the kitchen for water but returned holding money. "Someone must have stayed here last night and used our coffee pot. I found three one-hundred-dollar bills on the kitchen island."

"Are the intruders gone?" Jameson asked.

"I checked outside. There aren't any boats," Nicholas said.

"I suppose there was no harm in them sheltering here for the night." Jameson removed his rain cloak and folded it over his arm, glad he hadn't been home to startle those seeking shelter from the storm. "I don't know about you two, but I'm changing out of these wet clothes."

They all agreed and met in the living room after donning fresh shirts and pants. Jameson led Sloan to a sofa and draped her with a chenille blanket. She refused warm tea, too distraught to eat or drink.

Nicholas sat opposite her, tapping his finger on his temple. Within minutes, he jumped up and paced before the windows. "I need to saddle my horse and hunt for Vivi. She might have made it back to the bunker. I'll keep searching for as long as it takes to learn what happened to her." He dashed from the room, leaving Jameson and Sloan alone.

Appreciating the solo time with her, Jameson tucked the soft blanket under her chin. "There's much you don't understand." He jammed his hands deep in his pockets.

"I agree, but there's much you haven't shared." Sloan curled to face him. "Maybe it's time to open up."

Jameson gripped his abdomen and headed to the kitchen.

"How come you're not locking me in my room?" Sloan shouted from the sofa.

"It's no longer necessary," Jameson said over his shoulder.

Sloan didn't understand. What did he mean?

His heavy footsteps descended the stairs to the lower level. Within seconds, they stomped up the steps. Sloan and he collided when she entered the kitchen. "I see you've been in my locked room. Was it the reason you left the bunker in the middle of the night?" His lips twisted as though he were in pain. "Don't deny it. The door is ajar." Jameson staggered to the kitchen island and fell against it.

Sloan backed away, unsure of how he'd react to the situation. "We have plenty to discuss, like why you've lied to me, but first, are you in pain?" Her heart flooded with compassion for him despite his behavior.

"Would you please hand me the amber bottle in the drawer over there?" Jameson tilted his head toward the cabinets.

A dark amber bottle lay inside the lower one. Sloan brought it for him to examine. "Is this it—hydromorphone?"

"Yes." Jameson extended his palm for her. "Would you get me two pills, and water from the jug on the counter too?"

She found a glass in an upper cupboard and poured water for him. Jameson accepted the items and swallowed the pills.

"Tell me about your pain." Sloan moved to the other side of the marble island.

"I will in time, but I've delayed sharing something important with you. Please have a seat, and I'll explain everything."

Six padded stools rested under the spotless marble-topped island, a testament to Esther's immaculate cleaning skills. Worried that Jameson might lose his temper, Sloan slid onto the stool farthest from him.

"What I have to say will take a while." Jameson propped himself against the island.

"Go ahead. Tell me everything." Sloan scooted toward a kitchen cutlery set on the countertop. She wasn't sure what to expect from him and wanted quick access to something for protection.

Jameson let out a breath. "I wish I didn't have to share this. I'll start by saying that old Fella has roamed Paradise Island since before my staff and I arrived. He's always been a dangerous reptile who hid in the swampy jungle tributaries and survived on whatever crocodiles eat. I stocked the island with quail so he'd leave us alone." Jameson wiped his face with his palms.

"Several days ago, I shared with you what happened the night Veronica fled the mansion, and Nicholas went after her. But I didn't tell you the entire truth." Jameson traced the veining in the marble countertop as he spoke, his shaky voice betraying a reluctance to continue.

Sloan groaned under her breath. Was he filled with remorse over the deception she hadn't noticed until she entered the forbidden room? "You lied to me?" She hugged herself to stop the shivering. "Why didn't you share everything?"

"I lied to protect you from the truth. Veronica never left the island."

"I knew it. Do you have her locked somewhere in the mansion? Is she in the forbidden room somewhere— behind a hidden door?" Sloan leaned toward the cutlery set, hoping she wouldn't have to use it.

"Of course not. Nicholas and I are gentlemen. Because of what happened to Veronica, I banned communication and transportation from the island." Jameson bit his knuckle, hesitating before speaking again. "There's more to tell."

Sloan sensed the pain and sorrow in his voice. "I'm listening." She relaxed her shoulders, trying not to appear rigid.

"An unfortunate accident happened the night my fiancé fled the mansion. She ran straight to the beach, and Nicholas dashed after her. From my bedroom window, I heard him shout, 'Veronica, please allow Jameson to explain his condition. Don't run away. There's nowhere to go tonight. It's dark. We'll help you leave in the morning.'"

"But Veronica shouted, 'Jameson is a monster. He's hideous. I can't look at him.' She kept running, ignoring Nicholas, but every word resonated in my head long afterward." Jameson gulped the water in his glass.

"It was a pitch-dark night," he continued. "She tripped on a branch and landed head first into a log. When Nicholas reached her, she was unconscious. He ran to the barn and hooked up his steed to the wagon, planning to bring her back to the mansion, but when he returned, she was gone." Jameson raked back the hair from his forehead and clutched it in an iron grip, failing to release it.

"Where did she go?"

"I'm getting to that. My brother checked the Boyds' and Sims' home, thinking she'd fled there, but they denied seeing her. Even though Nicholas searched the shoreline for hours, he never found her. At sunrise, we returned to the beach in our night attire, me covered in head bandages, barely able to see. We found Veronica's teal scarf on a path leading to the jungle. Marks in the sand showed a struggle followed by drag marks. But we never found her body."

"Oh, my gosh, did…" Sloan covered her mouth. The wheels in her brain conjured an image too gruesome to imagine.

"After we all searched the island for days, we came to the same conclusion. Old Fella."

"You mean, he…he…"

"We'll never know for sure." Jameson released his hair, but his arms tensed as he braced them on the counter, using them for crutches to keep from falling. "We still search for her every time we hike the trails."

Sloan couldn't stop thinking about the croc snapping its jaw shut inches from her foot. She'd come so close to Veronica's fate. *What if Jameson hadn't arrived when he did?*

"Old Fella has evaded us, but we planned to put him down when we found him. The whole situation was traumatic for all of us, especially for Nicholas and me. I lost my fiancé and my self-esteem in one night. Because of Veronica's harsh words, I banned mirrors from the mansion. For years, I was a lit firecracker ready to explode at the least provocation."

Jameson's anger seemed appropriate, given the circumstances. *Was this what Nicholas meant by his brother's anger?* If Vivi suffered a similar fate, Sloan would react the same way.

"Veronica's horrible situation gripped me for a long time. Nicholas and I were so panic-stricken we dressed in our Marine fatigues and rode our horses to the beach whenever boaters came near the island. We shot bullets in the air to scare them away. We couldn't chance anyone meeting Veronica's fate."

"You and Nicholas are noble men."

"Caribbean gossip must have done its job because boats avoided our island after a few years. But we still carry pistols when we leave the house—to put Old Fella down if we spot him."

"Jameson, we have to find Vivi."

"We can saddle the horses when you feel up to it. But we'll have to take the long route because downed branches cover the trail."

"Let's go," Sloan said, heading to the rear door. "Are there more crocodiles on the island?"

"None that we've seen, but we don't take chances." Jameson removed his rain cloak from a hook near the back door and handed one to Sloan.

She donned hers, but her chest rose and fell as she met Jameson's eyes. "I need to know why you locked me in my room." She didn't mean to be so blunt, but she had to know.

A pained expression lined his face. "Initially, it was because Dr. Boyd told us activity might worsen your brain injury. All we needed was his okay for you to roam the mansion. After you tried to leave our home twice, Nicholas and I panicked. We feared you'd try again and succumb to Old Fella's jaws. Crocodiles have powerful legs and can outrun their prey. I guess we were right to worry. Thankfully, we found you in time today."

"But why didn't you alert me about Old Fella prowling the island? I would've stayed inside." Sloan earnestly searched his face for the truth.

Jameson paled as he gripped her shoulders. "I asked Nicholas to tell you. Didn't he?"

"He did after Dr. Boyd returned me to the mansion, but I thought he was trying to scare me into never leaving the house again."

"Nicholas suspected you'd think it was a scare tactic. That's why we refused to take a chance on you suffering Veronica's fate. Her entire accident devastated us. Can't you imagine losing your fiancé, your greatest love, in such a traumatic way?" Jameson turned away from her.

"It must have been a crushing blow." Sloan placed her hand on his back, hoping to ease his emotional suffering. "I'm so sorry for your loss."

Jameson wiped his mouth as though removing the bitter aftertaste from his ordeal. "Let's head to the barn. We need to find your sister." He opened the door for Sloan, but she hesitated to step outside.

"Wait, Jameson." She squared her shoulders. "Why did you deny having communication or transportation off the island?"

The muscles in Jameson's jaw tensed as if the questioning forced secrets to the surface that he'd hidden for years. "I had to keep my staff from leaving the island. What would I do if they abandoned me? They're all I have, Sloan." He turned his head from her. "They signed contracts to care for me until I pass, which might not be long, considering my frequent, intense pain."

After a few seconds, he sighed and faced her. "Nicholas has the key to my lockbox. I placed several items in it—my will, the key to the forbidden room, over a billion dollars for them to split, and deeds to various items. My staff will have instant access to everything—no waiting for the will to be read or for a bank to release the funds. And Nicholas will inherit my shares from our parents' pharmaceutical company. He'll never lack for anything and can do as he pleases. Dr. Boyd was a pilot in the Air Force before becoming a doctor, so I deeded him and Ivy the helicopter and Herb and Esther the yacht."

"How will Nicholas leave the island?" Sloan didn't like to persist, but she wanted answers while Jameson supplied them.

"I hope he'll stay and manage it. If he desires to leave, he can ride with Dr. Boyd or Herb to the mainland. I'm sure he'll purchase transportation when he's ready to return."

"There's one more thing bothering me." Sloan settled her hands at her waist. "Why didn't you allow Vivi to visit me?"

"I'll admit, it was more than just your head injury, although Dr. Boyd feared too much activity might cause brain swelling. The more I came to know you, the deeper I fell for your gentle spirit."

Sloan had used those very words about him.

"When Vivi told the Boyds you were in love with a guy named Rob, it upset me. I feared Vivi might encourage your relationship with him. She demanded a visit with you after she and Nicholas fell in love, but I couldn't bear it and deferred your meeting for as long as possible. The hurricane came along and settled it."

A horse and wagon clattered over the storm debris in the yard before rolling to a stop.

Sloan looked Jameson in the face, then charged outside.

Chapter Fifty

Jameson reached Sloan in the yard and placed his arm around her. He steadied her as they waited for the horse to stop. A blanket covered the wagon. Sloan gasped. "Did Nicholas find Vivi on the trail?" She plastered the back of her hand over her lips to safeguard a scream.

Nicholas leaped from his perch. "I found her!" His expressionless face gave no clues as to what lay under the blanket.

"Vivi?" Sloan gripped Jameson's hand so hard he flinched.

"Yes," Nicholas said. She reached the bunker, but Old Fella never crossed her path." Nicholas walked to the blanket.

Vivi removed it from her head. "I'm fine, Sloan." She climbed off the bedspreads beneath her and jumped from the wagon. "I'm just tired."

Sloan embraced her with an unyielding grip. Her sister meant the world to her. "How did you lose your shoes, Viv?"

"The heel broke off one, so I kicked them both aside. Nicholas came searching for me and shared what happened with Old Fella. I'm so sorry you encountered

the crocodile." She kissed her sister's cheek. "I could have lost you."

"I'm thankful Old Fella didn't find you because I couldn't bear losing you again." Sloan pressed her cheek to Vivi's.

"Would you mind my interrupting?" Jameson asked. "I need some alone time with Sloan." He tugged her hand. "I have something to tell you."

Was this about the forbidden room? Couldn't he let it go?

Chapter Fifty-One

Sloan wasn't sure if she could handle more information. Jameson had maxed her quota for shockers in one day. The wind whipped her face as she stopped on the beach to study the horizon. Light gray clouds laced the sky. How long until the storm would subside entirely? She longed for suntanning, swimming, and learning to surf if Jameson or Nicolas would teach her.

What was she thinking? Devoting more time to Jameson would complicate matters. She had to fly home.

"Do you mind if we stop here?" Jameson lowered to the sand on one knee.

He wouldn't propose, would he? Sloan covered her mouth and watched him scoop shells, stand, and toss one at a time into the waves. Her body relaxed as she waited for what he wanted to discuss.

After throwing his last shell, he strolled with her along the sand, his hair flying behind him in the wind. In a subtle motion, he wove his arm around her waist, and she let hers fall around his. In time, they reached a broken log. "Would you mind having a seat?" he asked.

"Is this the log where Veronica…"

"No, no, no. We removed it, Trust me." Jameson straddled the log and faced Sloan.

She couldn't help but study his appearance. The bronze prosthesis blended with his tanned skin until it nearly became invisible. And despite the injuries, his tawny hair, highlighted by luminous rays during years spent surfing, framed his face in a pleasing manner. She no longer noticed the jagged scar because the brown eye patch lent him a mysterious appeal.

"Sloan, I don't know how to begin except to offer the truth."

She snapped from her musings. "Jameson, don't—"

"I have to, Sloan. Ever since you washed up on the beach, I've loved you and hoped you might love me in return some day."

Sloan's heart began racing. Kindness radiated from Jameson as he spoke. He'd carried heavy burdens from his parents' deaths, the gunshot wounds to his face, and what happened to Veronica, yet Sloan had misjudged him. She'd thought he was a lunatic and cruel when he'd only been trying to protect her from Old Fella the best way he knew how. How could she break his heart?

Memories of Rob suddenly surfaced, distracting her from Jameson. She had belly-laughed with Rob, and their long work days flew by despite handling cardiac emergencies. She nibbled her bottom lip, deep in thought. If Rob liked her, wouldn't he have flown with her to the Caribbean? If he had, she and Vivi wouldn't have taken the puddle jumper. And she and Rob might have developed more than a working relationship during their seven-day tropical vacation. Given he was the first man she ever loved, his memory would forever come between her and Jameson.

"Sloan, will you marry me?" Jameson's earnest plea wavered between hope and unease.

Tears pricked her eyes. She couldn't deny the romantic sparks generated by his attempted kisses, nor her doubts because of his lies. Could she ever trust him again? Her heart ached with the enormous weight of a reply. Would his broken soul survive a refusal?

"Please, Sloan, don't deny me your love." He clutched his abdomen. "I have little time left on this earth. Marry me. You'll become a billionaire, and I'll receive my greatest joy, my dying wish—to pass from this world with your lips touching mine."

"I'm flattered by your love for me, Jameson, and I admire how you valiantly rescued fellow Marines, but we don't know each other well enough." Torn between her loyalty to Rob and her burgeoning affection for Jameson, she feared making the wrong choice.

The clouds darkened and a light rain fell as they lingered. "We'd better head back." Jameson offered her his hand and assisted her to her feet, then clutched his abdomen and doubled over. "The pain has flared again. I need to hurry to the mansion."

As they turned against the wind and rain, Jameson fell to his knees, gripping his belly. "The pain is much worse. I can't go on."

Sloan kneeled beside him and scanned the surroundings for a way to help him. His face had paled and his skin was now clammy. She spotted a log the storm had hurled on the beach and rolled it under his legs to raise them higher than his head, then she tore her shirt hem, soaked it with seawater, and placed it over his brow. "Hang on, Jameson. I'll get help." She kissed his cheek then bolted toward the mansion.

Chapter Fifty-Two

More than an hour had passed since Rob and Delroy left the island. Light rain swept by a whistling wind was a welcomed sight compared to what they had endured for the last few days. Waves splashed against the dinghy, rocking it. Protected by the rain slicker and its hood, Rob sat on a bench as the vessel headed toward Scarlett Bay. But a sudden revelation struck him. "Sloan wrote HELP on the beach, Detective. I'd stake my life on it. It's time to return to the island."

"You might be right, boss. But the authorities should handle the situation. Remember, ex-Marines live here. You're not equipped."

Feeling helpless, Rob glanced over his shoulder at Delroy. "There has to be something we can do."

"Look!" Delroy nodded at a large boat hugging the coast of Paradise Island.

"Delroy, it's my yacht!"

"They might not have spotted us. Let's see what they're up to." The detective cut the motor as they watched the yacht drop anchor and lower a lifeboat into the water. Two men descended the ladder and jumped into the vessel. One man rowed toward Paradise Island while the other scanned the shoreline with binoculars.

"We're behind them. They haven't seen us," Rob whispered. "Let's row to shore and ensure they're not up to no good."

"It'll take us an hour to get there. Battling this current ain't going to be easy." Delroy released a heavy breath.

Rob handed him an oar. "How about we do it together?"

Chapter Fifty-Three

The mad dash to the mansion for help left Sloan drained of energy. Nicholas summoned the doctor on his Walkie-Talkie, and he and Herb brought Jameson home by wagon. After they carried him to bed, she tucked him under the covers and dropped on the overstuffed chair beside him.

Dr. Boyd palpated his abdomen. "Where's your pain?"

Jameson touched the area below his navel.

"Other than increasing your medication, I'm afraid there's nothing more I can do."

"Would surgery help?" Sloan bit her tongue to avoid spilling the truth about the forbidden room. It wasn't her place to inform the staff.

"Unfortunately, we don't have diagnostic machines, so I'm unable to run tests. There's no way for me to know what's going on internally."

An idea came to Sloan. "Would you mind allowing Jameson and me a private moment?"

The doctor took his leave and closed the door.

Sloan placed Jameson's hand in hers. "Please tell the doctor about your secret room. A surgeon might save your life if we get you to a hospital in time."

Wincing from pain, Jameson studied the ceiling. "I'm not sure I want to prolong my life. I've suffered mentally and physically for five long years. And my self-confidence and self-esteem barely exist because I'll never regain the same physical prowess I once had. Women used to vie for my attention. Can you imagine how devastating it was to lose such an important part of my life? The damage to my face has ruined me."

Sloan brushed the hair from his eyes. "Your attitude, more than your appearance, has ruined your outlook on life. I no longer notice your facial flaws because of your charming behavior. Yes, your behavior is still charming—your loving kindness and attention to the needs of others are valuable qualities. You're still attractive, Jameson, despite your accident. But hanging onto the past will destroy you. Let it go and accept your new life—the person you've become—one of the most desirable men I've ever met."

A tear slipped down Jameson's cheek. "Are you saying that to make me feel better?"

"I wouldn't lie to you. Tell Dr. Boyd about your forbidden room. Allow him to fly you to a hospital."

Their eyes met and Jameson's gaze spoke of his desire. "Only if you marry me first."

She tenderly squeezed his hand. If marrying Jameson would save his life, she had to mull it over. "I'll consider your proposal."

"If you don't marry me, I'll have no reason to live." Jameson gripped his belly and moaned.

The door creaked open.

Dr. Boyd entered, carrying a tray with pills and water. "I didn't want to disturb you, but I brought medicine." He raised Jameson's head and assisted him in taking four pills. "I know what's in your special room. As soon as the storm clears, I'll fly you to Florida."

Jameson swallowed the medicine. "How long have you known?"

"Since this morning. Vivi told us when she returned to the storm bunker. Why would you deceive your staff when we've dedicated our lives to helping you?"

"Could we discuss it when my pain eases?" Jameson curled into a ball. "Just know this—I was afraid my staff would abandon me."

"You and Nicholas have become like sons to us. We're family, and families don't abandon one another. Your brother and I believe surgery will offer the best odds for survival. We'll fly in the morning." The doctor closed his medical bag.

Sloan appreciated his advice. She'd do nearly anything to help Jameson. *But would it mean forgetting Rob?*

Chapter Fifty-Four

A knock struck the door. Sloan rose from her bed and walked to the sofa as Nicholas entered carrying red juice and fresh buttered bread. "Dr. Boyd will perform the ceremony in an hour," he said. "The doc's a licensed officiate. Afterward, he'll fly you and Jameson to a Florida emergency room. Every tick of the clock places his life in danger. We have to hurry."

"But I never agreed to marry him." A knot of fear tightened her gut as she cautiously sipped the juice. She needed time to process the situation.

"You know Jameson will refuse medical intervention unless you agree. Please, Sloan. He'll either receive a chance at life or die in my arms on this island."

Sloan stared into space, an uneasiness squeezing her temples. "I care about Jameson, but I love another man. Are you asking me to give up my first love?"

"I'm sorry, but yes, I'm asking you to marry my brother. I'll do anything to save him. He's all I have left in this world except for Vivi." Nicholas slid beside Sloan on the sofa. His swollen eyes pleaded with her to comply. "Dr. Boyd called a hospital in the United States. The Emergency Room will run diagnostic tests, and if indicated, Jameson will have surgery," he added.

"But I'm not sure I can marry him." Sloan drank half the juice and set the glass on the tray.

"Miss, I beg you to see Jameson through this. We don't know if surgery will help. He might die. And if he does, you'll become an instant billionaire. You can marry whomever you please." He eyed her half-empty glass.

Dizziness clouded her thinking. The red juice. It was the same juice Esther had given her. Sloan spotted something hanging from the en suite door—a white wedding gown shimmering in the bright morning light. Her heart raced. Someone had been in her room during the night. She staggered to the bathroom and inspected the dress before stumbling around to face Nicholas. "What is this doing here? I haven't agreed to marry Jameson."

Nicholas avoided her gaze, his focus on the gown. "You're stuck on this island. There's nowhere to go unless we allow it. I'm so sorry, but you have no other choice."

She gazed out the window, pondering a response. After several seconds, she reeled around. "No one can bully me into marrying him."

Nicholas glared at her with fire in his eyes. "Esther and Ivy Boyd will ensure your compliance."

Sloan's heart sank. She had no way to stop them. They had her trapped like a goldfish in a glass jar. "Do I have a choice?"

"No, ma'am." Nicholas exited the room and closed the door behind him.

Powerless and afraid, Sloan climbed on her bed. Sobbing, she buried her face in a pillow. What was she to do? Answers failed her. Her eyelids fluttered as her head drooped.

Nicholas had put something in her drink.

Esther entered Sloan's room unannounced, followed by Ivy Boyd. They assisted her to the edge of her four-poster bed. "How is the young bride coming along?" Esther's face glowed with excitement.

"Please. Don't. Call me. That." Groggy from the medicine, Sloan's words tumbled out thick from the effects of the drug.

"Are you not feeling well, dear?" Ivy's comforting voice made up for Esther's exuberance.

"Nicholas. Drugged. Me."

"Now, now. Nicholas only wants what's best for his brother." Ivy gripped Sloan's shoulders and looked into her eyes. "Are you having doubts about marriage?"

"It's just…I–I–I never agreed to this." Sloan bunched the sheet under her fingers. What was happening to her? She couldn't think clearly. "There's someone I love… before the plane crash, he…." Her thick tongue made speaking difficult.

Esther placed her arms around Sloan in a snug embrace. "Don't worry. You're not alone. We all have doubts on our wedding day. It's natural. But Jameson is a wonderful man."

Sloan released a jagged breath. "But what of his temper?"'

"There's nothing to worry about. Veronica's tragic death affected him. Wouldn't it devastate any fiancé? His temper flared. The slightest thing set him off. But he had no hope for a future back then." Esther placed her hand on Sloan's arm. "Losing Veronica depressed him, and depressed people often have short fuses. When you arrived on this island, it renewed his hope for a new life, and he protected you from the vicious crocodile the only

way he knew how. Can you forgive him? His temper has been under control for more than a year."

Ivy walked to the en suite and removed the delicate dress from the hanger. "Have you seen this yet?" She carried the gown to the bedside.

The shimmering sleeveless gown blended elegance with simplicity.

"Who did it belong to?" Sloan feared the answer she might receive.

"It doesn't matter." Esther motioned for Sloan to follow her. "Come and try it on. It'll look gorgeous on you."

Sloan stood and staggered a few steps, trying not to crumple in her lethargic state. Esther and Ivy rushed to place their shoulders under her arms and escorted her to the en suite.

Ivy assisted her in removing her night clothes and helped her don the gown as Esther steadied her frail body. The V-neck dress hung on Sloan's frame. She gasped when she spied her thin image in the mirror.

The reflection before Sloan was that of a sun-deprived, frightened woman in an oversized wedding gown. How could she escape this mess?

"What do you think?" Esther held Sloan's trembling hands.

Sloan's smile deflated like her ruined dreams. *How could she marry the perplexing recluse who harbored far too many secrets and enjoyed isolation?* She'd never adjust to his world.

"It'll be okay," Esther said. "We'll help you get through this."

"Herb should have the bouquets ready for the ceremony by now." Ivy glanced at her watch. "We can't be late."

As Ivy brushed Sloan's silky hair, Esther slipped her sandals on her feet.

Whatever medication Nicholas had given Sloan rendered her tongue and her body a rubbery mess. Esther and Ivy wove their arms in hers and escorted her from the room to the beach.

Jameson and Dr. Boyd waited under a trellis covered in the most beautiful wildflowers growing on the island. Nicholas stood to his right as the best man, Herb, as a groomsman. Someone started the CD player, and "Just the Way You Are" began playing.

Carrying a pink rose bouquet, Vivi strolled down the makeshift wooden aisle covered in folded satin sheets scattered with pink petals. Holding an identical bouquet, Ivy stepped behind her.

"Are you ready?" When Sloan didn't respond, Esther handed her a beautiful white lily bouquet. Esther girded her side like a steel beam as they headed down the aisle together.

Dressed in beige pants and a pale sage shirt, Jameson waited for her beneath the archway. The sage accented his flowing hair. When Sloan reached the arch, Esther held her upright on the left, and Jameson propped her on the right.

With everyone in place, Dr. Boyd initiated the ceremony. "Good morning, family. We're here today to celebrate a joyous occasion—the joining of our friends who are united in mind, spirit, and purpose. I think I'm expressing Jameson and Sloan's desires for their marriage when I say 'love and respect for one another will take priority above all else.' We're a family on this island, and we'll embrace their union with immense love."

Sloan studied her feet as he spoke. Was she doing the right thing, or should she speak up and resist?

Dr. Boyd continued, "I'll keep this brief in order to fly my patient to the hospital." He glanced at Jameson. "Do

you take this woman, Sloan Lauren Evans, for your lawfully wedded wife…"

When the doctor finished reading the groom's vows, Jameson said, "I do."

Dr. Boyd turned to Sloan. "Do you take this man…

Chapter Fifty-Five

Sloan swayed in the fitted bridal gown, her silky espresso hair cascading over her shoulders. Dr. Boyd repeated the question she most dreaded. "Do you take this man, Jameson Branson Briggs, as your lawfully wedded husband?"

Sloan's world spun before her eyes. If she responded with the two tiny words Jameson yearned to hear, they'd forever change her life. Esther tightened the grip on her arm as she gazed at the shoreline bathed in dismal clouds and raindrops. The waves had almost calmed from the storm, but seawater sprayed her face. The cool, salty water awakened her. She straightened and attempted to remove Esther's hands. If only she could bolt to the water and flee.

Before making a critical marriage decision, Sloan needed time to weigh the positives and negatives associated with Jameson and Rob. Her eyes misted as she pondered their merits. Both men were charming, tender, and kind. Choosing Jameson would make her a billionaire, but it would also mean she had to spend her entire life on Paradise Island with a recluse. Despite his injuries, she admired and perhaps loved him until her memories of Rob surfaced. The brilliant, fun-loving cardiothoracic surgeon was the man she adored.

She inhaled deeply, stalling over her decision. As she prepared to answer Dr. Boyd, two disheveled figures climbed from a dinghy in the distance. The men raced toward the ceremony, kicking up sand. One man wore a red and yellow striped hat over ginger hair. He stopped short at the floral arch.

Sloan recognized the man without a doubt. *Trinidad.*

She worked harder to pry Esther's grip from her arm, but Esther clamped her fingers tighter. Sloan had a question for the despicable pilot. Why hadn't he directed the boat captain to save her and Vivi when the bearded man rescued him? Vivi had been conscious after the crash, and she shared about the captain deliberately leaving her and Sloan behind.

"What do we have here?" Trinidad asked the group. "Is someone getting married?" His scratchy voice dripped with malice. "Where is Jameson Briggs?"

A bald man with snake tattoos arrived at the floral arch and grabbed Jameson's arm. "This man looks like the one in the picture."

Perspiration covered Jameson's brow as he clutched his abdomen and sputtered, "I–I…"

"Leave him alone! I'm Jameson Briggs," Nicholas shouted.

"I doubt it. You look like a picture of his brother." The bald man's gold earring dangled as he seized Nicholas with his free hand. "Let's take them both. I'm betting their pharmaceutical company will pay hefty ransoms for their hides."

"Well, looky here. This is our big day." Trinidad grabbed Sloan around the waist as she tried to run. "This here's the lady who went down in my plane. And there's her sister. We've hit the jackpot." He pulled a pistol from under his shirt and aimed it at them. "Don't plan on running."

With lightning speed, Nicholas produced a pistol from his waistband and struggled with his bald captor. His gun went off, shooting the man in the foot. The man screeched and dropped to the sand, gripping his shin and crying out in pain.

Trinidad directed his gun at Nicholas. "Don't anybody move."

Nicholas raised his arms as a second dinghy appeared near the first one on the beach. A towering man with broad shoulders lumbered up the sand with a leaner man close behind.

"Put that gun down unless you have someone to write your obituary," the towering man shouted to Trinidad. He pointed a gun at the pilot's chest.

Head down, Jameson plowed into Trinidad's side. Trinidad shrieked and fell to the sand. The towering man reached the pilot as he attempted to stand and booted him to his back. "You ain't going nowhere, pal."

Jameson moaned and gripped his abdomen before falling alongside Trinidad. He raised on an elbow, clutched his side, and brandished a pistol he had removed from his waistband. "I'm Jameson Briggs, ex-Marine Forces Special Ops. Drop your gun and identify yourself," he said to the behemoth man.

A smile curved the big man's lips. "I'm Special Ops, 2nd Battalion, 5th Marines, Sigmund Arthur Delroy, sir." He beamed as he lowered his weapon.

Jameson squinted at the man. "First Lieutenant?"

"Yes, sir."

"Art Delroy saved my life and risked his own when he carried me to the chopper after my injuries." Jameson looked up at Delroy from where he lay on the sand. "I never imagined I'd see you again."

"It was an honor serving under you, Captain Briggs." Delroy saluted Jameson. "I didn't know this was your island."

Trinidad tugged his Rastafarian hat in place. "It's hard to pull off a good scam these days. Everyone knows someone."

A man with dark hair emerged from behind Delroy. "You're right, Trinidad." The man raked the dark, ratty hair from his eyes.

Sloan recognized the voice and the action. "Rob?" Was it him? The man before her didn't resemble the stylish doctor she adored.

He eyed the floral arch, wedding aisle, and scattered bouquets on the ground. "What's going on here? Are you getting married, Sloan?"

"Yes…no. I mean, I'll have to explain." She searched his face for the man she'd fallen in love with. Beneath the scruffy beard, sea-soaked clothes, and wild, unwashed hair, she spotted an Ambrose dimple and rushed into his arms. "Rob, where have you been?"

"Looking for you." His smile stretched to the sea and back, and he spun her around, gripping her waist like he'd never let go. "I knew I'd find you."

The beam on Delroy's face lit the dismal sky.

The noisy whir of a police helicopter announced its landing on an isolated stretch of the beach. The wedding party along with the criminals watched as an officer jumped to the sand.

Huffing and puffing, Dr. Boyd ran to the chopper from behind a dune. "Come this way, Officer. I'll show you to the perpetrators."

"Ah, you must've been the guy who called us." Diaz's eagle eyes scanned the fallen and those surrounding them. The policeman touched his holster when he spotted the criminals. "We've been looking for you, Trinidad. And you, too, Kingfish."

"Well, we ain't been lookin' for you, Diaz." Like a scammer caught in the act, Kingfish hung his head and sunk his hands deep in his pockets.

Diaz placed his thumbs in his waist band. "I'd like to say I dislike taking you two in, but that'd be a lie, now, wouldn't it?"

"All depends on who you're talking to," Kingfish said. "Plenty of people know I'm innocent."

"That'll be the day," Delroy said.

Using zip-ties, the officer secured Trinidad's and Kingfish's wrists behind their backs then made the rounds on the beach, taking statements from those present. When they finished with the details, the officer closed his notepad and placed the pen in his pocket. "Will you assist Kingfish to the chopper, Detective Delroy? His foot doesn't appear to be working right, just like his mouth."

"I'd be glad to help." Delroy supported Kingfish under his arm, and the ex-convict hopped the distance on one foot. "Looks like you'll be behind bars again." Delroy nudged him into the chopper.

"Don't rub it in," Kingfish replied.

Diaz prodded Trinidad into the aircraft. "Would you mind riding with us to Jamaica, Detective? I have more questions."

"No problem. But before we leave, I'd like to ask Trinidad something."

"Sure, fire away when ready." The officer stood aside.

Delroy's nostrils flared as he struggled for a breath before whistling its slow release. "I'd give two cents to know how you started the yacht."

"Two cents? Is that all you've got?" Trinidad turned his head and stared at the sand dune. "I'm not giving away my secrets. I'll be spending enough time behind bars."

"Did you hear that, boss?" Delroy shouted to Rob.

Rob grimaced at Trinidad's words. "Nice try, Delroy." He dangled the keys from his yacht. "I kept these, so we're good. Thank you for helping me find Sloan. I couldn't have done it without you."

Delroy saluted Rob with two fingers before accepting Officer Diaz's outstretched hand and climbing into the chopper.

Out on the sea, a police boat intercepted Rob's yacht. Rob had reported Trinidad and his gang for stealing it when he gave his statement to Officer Diaz. Diaz called in the theft over his radio.

As the chopper departed, Sloan shouted to Dr. Boyd, "Who alerted the police in the first place?"

"Jameson deserves the credit. He pointed at the mansion. I ran to the house and called the police from the forbidden room. You might offer the precinct a huge donation, Jameson." Dr. Boyd clapped him on the back before adding, "I'll bring the wagon around. Nicholas and I will have you on your private chopper to the ER in no time."

"I'm coming too." Vivi clutched Nicholas's hands. "I'm not letting this hunk out of my sight."

Like a man in love, Nicholas lifted her chin and kissed her. "You'll never have to worry, Viv. We're getting married soon."

Rob slipped his hand around Sloan's waist, and she rested her head on his shoulder. "I don't know how you did it, Rob, but I'm so glad you found me."

Languishing on the sand, Jameson rolled to his back. "I guess this means you're not marrying me, Sloan."

She released Rob's hand and folded to her knees beside Jameson, searching for the right words to ease his suffering. "I'm so sorry. I never wanted to hurt you." She stroked his clenched jaw. "Before Vivi shared details with me last night, I didn't remember my past. Now that I do, I need to follow my heart."

"But I hoped you'd choose me." Jameson curled on his side, gripping his abdomen.

Sloan swept the hair from his eyes. "After your story about Veronica, I understood about my locked room, but I wish you'd told me the truth when I washed ashore." She warmed his icy hands in hers. "Your kind nature drew me in, but I fell in love with Rob two years ago. I hope you'll find someone who loves you as much as you loved Veronica." She wrapped him in a heartfelt hug. "Follow the doctor's orders and heal from the inside and out."

"I'll never forget you, Sloan." Jameson squeezed her hands.

Wagon wheels and horse-hooves sprayed the air with sand as Dr. Boyd reined them to a halt on the beach. Nicholas and Vivi sprang into action. They assisted Jameson to a comfortable position in the wagon's bed then jumped aboard with him.

Sloan pressed her cheek to Jameson's one last time before Dr. Boyd nodded to her. She moved away as the horses galloped back to the mansion. Salty tears stung her eyes. Yet a peace came over her as she wiped them away. The hospital in Florida would provide Jameson with better odds of survival than he'd have on Paradise Island. Valiant Jameson Briggs, who placed her needs and those of his fellow soldiers above his own, deserved a better life.

When the wagon disappeared behind a dune, Sloan strolled to a log farther up the beach, where Rob waited for her. He rose and intertwined his fingers in hers when she stood before him. "Losing a friend is difficult, Sloan, but choosing between two men must have been a challenge." He gently swept the hair from her face behind her ear. "Ever since you left for Scarlett Bay, I've wondered what you wanted to ask me…in the airport parking lot."

Judging by his disheveled appearance, Rob had quite a journey searching for her, so the least she could do was to tell the truth. She cleared her throat and took a deep breath. "I wanted to ask if we could spend time together on the island. I've hoped for more than a doctor/nurse relationship for two long years."

Rob lifted her pale hand and kissed it as though it was the finest porcelain. "It's what I've wanted for months." His arms circled her thin waist, and she melted into his warm embrace. "Isn't this the point where snowball-throwing teens interrupted us in the parking lot?" A grin trickled over his lips.

"I believe so." Sloan broke into a smile. "But how did you find me on Paradise Island?"

"The scattered tree branches on the sand. Somehow, I knew they were a message from you."

The tears that hadn't stopped flowing for a good part of the morning blurred Sloan's vision. "I never thought I'd see you again."

"I never stopped looking for you from the moment we parted. I'm hopelessly in love with you, Sloan. That's what I wanted to say in the airport. I wanted to tell you how I felt. I'll never let another day go by without you."

"I love you, too, Rob, and I always will."

Sloan raised on her toes and gazed deeply into his lake blue eyes, the dreamy portals to his soul. Cupping his head, she pulled him in, her lips meeting his—feathery light at first—followed by a fiery fusion that would last an eternity because she'd never let go.

Epilogue

Paradise Island, 2018

The sun's brilliant rays poured through the quaint chapel, bathing the altar and pews in a warm glow. Immense joy filled Sloan as she stood in the sanctuary and admired the earthy stone structure Nicholas had built for Vivi. When people began assembling there for Sunday worship, he hired a full-time minister to lead the congregation. It had been a couple years since Sloan departed the island, and so much had changed. The original staff had stayed on, but not as workers. They were a family who cherished and supported one another.

Nicholas and Vivi had married after Jameson recovered from surgery, and upon returning to Paradise Island, they settled in the mansion. Many people from Florida and elsewhere purchased land on the island. Some built homes and others had theirs under construction.

Nicholas became the first governor. The islanders appreciated his kindness and generosity. Giant construction machines brought in by barges cut down the jungle and replaced it with streets and shops.

Electricity, phone towers, and a transportation depot were in various stages of completion.

Trinidad, Kingfish, Easy Joe, and Captain Reynauld received steep sentences for their crimes, but Mac avoided incarceration with a plea bargain after confessing the entire plot and naming those involved. She received a six-month house arrest for her part in the scheme.

Days before Sloan arrived with Rob on the island, he called Cal, who happened to be in St. Anne's Landing. The pilot flew them to the small domestic airport in Scarlett Bay. Cal had purchased the airport and placed Clive on the payroll as their mechanic. He also hired a St. Anne's Landing pilot to take turns with him flying Caribbean tourists and islanders to their local destinations.

Delroy had retired from detective work and now lived on his yacht—the one Rob had deeded him for saving everyone on the island two years ago. When Delroy learned Rob and Sloan had returned to Scarlett Bay, he insisted on sailing them to Paradise Island, but Rob refused his offer and brought Sloan to the island in the dinghy he'd used for her rescue. On their arrival, joyous laughter pealed from Esther, Herb, Ivy, Dr. Boyd, Nicholas, and Vivi—the original Paradise Island residents—everyone but Jameson, who hadn't returned to the island, having devised a tale of his own.

Sloan checked the clock on the church balcony. Esther, Ivy, and Vivi were on their way to the church to help her prepare for the wedding.

An hour later, Sloan cracked the dressing room door and studied the wedding guests assembling in the church.

A man with shoulder-length tawny hair strode down the aisle with a gorgeous woman on his arm. A faint, almost imperceptible scar wove down his face, but he possessed two eyes and a slender nose prosthesis that blended with his skin. Jameson had corresponded with Sloan and kept her abreast of his endeavors. His abdominal surgery had been a success. His surgeon removed a cancerous tumor and subsequent medication courses healed him.

She smiled because he'd heeded her advice and agreed to the plastic surgery. Even though it repaired his features, Sloan knew he was no longer the same young man he had been before the gunshot to his face. What he'd lived through made him an amazing man and far more desirable than he could have imagined. She admired him for so many reasons.

During his time in America, he had met the chestnut-haired beauty, Isabelle, who loved him more than he believed possible. Sloan never doubted women would chase him once his attitude about his self-image changed. He possessed many outstanding qualities and accomplished every one of the challenges she'd given him.

Today, after months of therapy for agoraphobia, he made the trip to Paradise Island to celebrate Sloan's wedding.

The petite Isabelle glued to Jameson's side radiated love and devotion for him as they walked down the aisle. He clutched her hand in his as he located available seats and assisted her into a pew. Sloan's heart warmed at the sight.

A few minutes passed before the groomsmen, Nicholas, Ethan, Gray Addington, and Delroy, dressed in matching white shorts and pastel blue shirts, filed into the sanctuary and flanked Rob at the altar. Beaming with happiness, Rob fiddled with his silver collared top as he waited for Sloan to join him.

Organ music began playing, and Sloan's bridesmaids, arrayed in strapless silver gowns, carried pink bouquets down the aisle. Vivi, the maid of honor, sported a baby bump, and Lainie Vanderhuel, Sloan's best friend from the cardiology clinic, dazzled the guests with her magnificent diamond engagement ring from Ethan. Saige Addington and another of Sloan's childhood friends walked the aisle behind them.

When the last bridesmaid reached the altar, Ivy placed a stunning lily bouquet in Sloan's hands and pushed a button on the CD player. Rob had insisted on selecting the wedding song as a tribute to Sloan. At the rehearsal dinner, he had gushed that she was his cherished second chance at love. She had no idea which song he chose.

"Perfect" by Ed Sheeran began playing, and tears welled in Sloan's eyes. Dazed by Rob's selection, she became lost in a sea of love for the man who never stopped searching for her after the plane crash. Ivy finally nudged her to begin walking.

Breathtaking in a white strapless, empire-waist bridal gown with a pastel blue sash, Sloan stepped down the aisle, escorted by her adoptive father. She lingered with him in front of the church until the music ended, and she and the starry-eyed romantics dabbed their eyes. Filled with joy and unquestionable love, she stepped to the altar, folded her hand in Rob's, and married the man of her dreams.

Dear reader

Thank you for your support and purchase of Find Me In Paradise. Now that you've finished reading, would you kindly write a review to let fellow readers know whether to check it out? Please go to Amazon and write your thoughts while the story is fresh in your mind. It'll take less than a minute of your time. Thank you!

ABOUT THE AUTHOR

Deb Gardner Allard is a retired registered nurse with an additional degree in psychology. She lives near beautiful Lake Michigan with her husband and impish Chihuahuas, Farley and Moosie.

When she's not reading or writing, she kicks back with Hallmark movies. Their cheerful music, upbeat storylines, and happy endings keep her smiling.

www.ingramcontent.com/pod-product-compliance
Lightning Source LLC
Chambersburg PA
CBHW030653260626

47157CB00007B/2621